JOYCE CAROL OATES

BLACK WATER

A WILLIAM ABRAHAMS BOOK

DUTTON

DUTTON

Published by the Penguin Group
Penguin Books USA Inc., 375 Hudson Street, New York, New York
10014, U.S.A.
Penguin Books Ltd, 27 Wrights Lane, London W8 5TZ, England
Penguin Books Australia Ltd, Ringwood, Victoria, Australia
Penguin Books Canada Ltd, 10 Alcorn Avenue, Toronto, Ontario,
Canada M4V 3B2
Penguin Books (N.Z.) Ltd, 182–190 Wairau Road, Auckland 10,
New Zealand

Penguin Books Ltd, Registered Offices:
Harmondsworth, Middlesex, England

First published by Dutton, an imprint of New American
Library, a division of Penguin Books USA Inc.
Distributed in Canada by McClelland & Stewart Inc.

First Printing, May, 1992
1   3   5   7   9   10   8   6   4   2

A portion of this novel first appeared in a different form in
Lear's, September 1991.

REGISTERED TRADEMARK—MARCA REGISTRADA

LIBRARY OF CONGRESS CATALOGING-IN-PUBLICATION DATA:
Oates, Joyce Carol, 1938–
Black water / Joyce Carol Oates.
p.   cm.
ISBN 0-525-93455-3
I. Title.
PS3565.A8B47   1992
813'.54—dc20   *91-40463*
                                                  CIP

Printed in the United States of America
Set in Garamond Book
Designed by Steven N. Stathakis

for the Kellys—

PART
ONE

1

THE RENTED TOYOTA, DRIVEN WITH SUCH IMPATIENT exuberance by The Senator, was speeding along the unpaved unnamed road, taking the turns in giddy skidding slides, and then, with no warning, somehow the car had gone off the road and had overturned in black rushing water, listing to its passenger's side, rapidly sinking.

Am I going to die?—like this?

2

IT WAS THE EVENING OF THE FOURTH OF JULY. ELSE-where on Grayling Island, along the northern shore in particular, there were parties, strings of cars parked along the narrow sandy roads leading to the beaches. Later, when it was sufficiently night, there would be fireworks, some of the displays lavish and explosive in brilliant Technicolor like the TV war in the Persian Gulf.

They were in a desolate unpopulated part of the Island, they were very possibly lost. She was framing her mouth, summoning her courage, to say the word *lost.*

As with the condom she'd been carrying in her purse for, how long. Her kidskin bag, and now her pretty floral-patterned Laura Ashley summer bag. In fact she'd carried it, the identical item, in an earlier bag as well—that big rakish straw bag with the red leather trim that finally fell to pieces she'd had it so long. The condom was neatly and tightly wrapped, it had a chaste pharmaceutical scent, it took up little space. Not once in these many months had she so much as touched it, preparatory to revealing it, preparatory to suggesting to whoever it was, whichever man, friend or professional acquaintance or near-stranger, that he use it, or even contemplate using it. You were prepared for any emergency but finally you could not speak, there were no words.

They were somewhere in the marshlands of Grayling Island, Maine, a twenty-minute ferry ride from Boothbay Harbor to the northwest. They had been talking companionably together, and they had been laughing easily together, like old friends, like the most casual of old friends, and Kelly was trying discreetly to steady The Senator's hand so that the remains of his vodka-and-tonic wouldn't splash over the rim of the plastic cup he held as he drove, and then, suddenly, as in a film when spasms like hiccups begin and the picture flies out of the frame, so suddenly, she would never comprehend how suddenly, the road flew out from beneath the rushing car and they were struggling for their lives sinking in black water splashing across the windshield seeking entry as if the dreamlike swampland on all sides had come now alive reaching up to devour them.

Am I going to die?—like this?

3

BUFFY HAD BEEN HURT OR HAD SEEMED SO. WITH Buffy, so much was display, you never knew. Saying to Kelly Kelleher, Yes but why leave *now*, can't you leave a little later?—and Kelly Kelleher mumbled something vague and embarrassed unable to say, Because he wants me to: he insists.

Unable to say, Because if I don't do as he asks there won't be any *later*. You know that.

4

On all sides a powerful brackish marshland odor, the odor of damp, and decay, and black earth, black water. The chill fresh stinging smell of the Atlantic seemed remote here, like memory, borne inland in thin gusts by an easterly wind. And no sound of the waves, here. Only the nocturnal insects. The wind in the stunted vine-laden trees.

Gripping the strap of the shoulder safety-harness Kelly Kelleher who was not drunk smiled thinking, How strange to be *here* yet not know where *here* is.

They were hurrying to get to the ferry in

Brockden's Landing, which would be leaving for the mainland at 8:20 P.M. It was approximately 8:15 P.M. when the rented Toyota unobserved by any witness plunged into the water—the creek? stream? river?—which neither The Senator nor his passenger Kelly Kelleher had known might be there at the apogee of a hairpin curve.

Approximately thirty feet ahead, unsighted too, was a narrow wooden bridge of badly weathered planks; but there had been no warning sign of a bridge, still less of the dangerous curve preceding the bridge.

Not now. Not like this.

She was twenty-six years eight months old too young to die thus too astonished, too disbelieving, to scream as the Toyota flew off the road and struck the surface of the near-invisible water as if for an instant it might not sink but float: as if the trajectory of its flight might carry it, the very weight of it, across the water and into the snaky tangle of rushes and stunted trees and vines on the farther shore.

You would expect water in such a place to be shallow, just a ditch. You would expect the guardrail to be more substantial. You would not expect to be, so suddenly so rudely so helplessly, in the water black as muck and smelling of raw sewage.

Not like this. No.

She was astonished, and she was disbelieving, and it may have been that The Senator too shared this reaction, for the Fourth of July on Grayling Island at Buffy St. John's parents' place had been celebratory and careless and marked by a good deal of laughter and spirited conversation and innocent excited anticipation of the future (both the immediate and the distant future—for, surely, one determines the other), thus it was virtually impossible to comprehend how its tone might change so abruptly.

Several times in her life Kelly Kelleher had experienced accidents of a similar abrupt and confusing nature and each time she had been rendered incapable of screaming and each time from the first instant of realizing herself out of control, the fate of her physical body out of the control of her brain, she had had no coherent perception of what in fact *was* happening.

For at such moments time accelerates. Near the point of impact, time accelerates to the speed of light.

Patches of amnesia like white paint spilling into her brain.

5

SHE HEARD, AS THE TOYOTA SMASHED INTO A GUARD-rail that, rusted to lacework, appeared to give way without retarding the car's speed at all, The Senator's single startled expletive—"Hey!"

And then the water out of nowhere flooding over them. Over the hood of the car. Over the cracked windshield. Churning in roiling waves as if alive, and angry.

6

AT BROWN UNIVERSITY, WHERE SHE HAD GRADUATED summa cum laude with a bachelor's degree in American Studies, Kelly Kelleher, baptismal name Elizabeth Anne Kelleher, had written her ninety-page senior honor's thesis on The Senator.

Its subtitle was "Jeffersonian Idealism and 'New Deal' Pragmatism: Liberal Strategies in Crisis."

She had worked very hard: researching The Senator's three campaigns for the Senate, his career in the Senate, his influence within the Democratic Party and the likelihood of his being nominated as his party's candidate for president,

and for her effort she had received a grade of *A*
... Kelly Kelleher's undergraduate grades in her
major were usually *A*'s ... and nearly a page of
handwritten commentary and praise from her
advisor.

This had been five years ago. When she'd
been young.

Meeting The Senator that afternoon, her
small-boned hand so vigorously shaken in his
big gregarious hand, Kelly instructed herself, Do
not bring the subject up.

And so she had not. Until much later.

When, things having developed so rapidly
as they had, it would have been to no purpose
not to.

Scorpio for the month of July, she, Buffy,
and Stacey had read giggling in the new *Glam-
our* the night before: *Too much caution in revealing your impulses and desires to others!
For once demand YOUR wishes and get YOUR
own way! Your stars are wildly romantic now,
Scorpio, after a period of disappointment—GO
FOR IT!*

Poor Scorpio, so easily bruised. So easily
dissuaded.

That sullen haughty look that so annoyed
Artie Kelleher, the father: that inward-gnawing
look that so worried Madelyn Kelleher, the
mother. *Yes I love you please will you let me
alone?*

Poor Scorpio, twenty-six years eight months old, yet susceptible, still, to adolescent skin problems! The ignominy of it, the rage. Her thin fair skin that was too thin, too fair. Those mysterious hives, rashes. Allergies inflaming her eyes. Yes and acne, near-invisible but gritty little pimples at her hairline ...

When her lover had loved her she'd been beautiful. When she'd been beautiful her lover had loved her. It was a simple proposition, a seemingly tautological proposition, yet it resisted full comprehension.

So, she would not try to comprehend it. She would embark upon a new life a new adventure a wildly romantic adventure, reckless Scorpio.

7

KELLY KELLEHER HAD TACTFULLY SUGGESTED THAT
The Senator turn on the Toyota's headlights, and
now as they made their way deeper into the
marshland following what appeared to be an
abandoned secondary road the headlights
bounced and careened with the car's speed since
The Senator, impatient, muttering under his
breath, was driving erratically swinging the car
along the bumpy road not minding how the remains of his vodka-and-tonic splashed over the
rim of the plastic cup, onto the seat and onto
Kelly Kelleher's thigh, the cotton-knit fabric of
her new summer shift. The Senator was what is

known as an aggressive driver and his adversary was the road, the gathering dusk, the distance between himself and his destination, and the rapidly shrinking quantity of time he had to get to that destination, pressing down hard and petulant on the gas pedal bringing the car's speed up to forty miles an hour, and then hitting the brakes going into a turn, and then pressing down hard on the gas pedal again so that the car's tires protested faintly spinning before taking hold in the sandy glutinous soil, and then hitting the brakes again. The giddy rocking motion of the car was like hiccups, or copulation.

The way, Kelly uneasily recalled, her father had sometimes driven after one of his and her mother's mysterious disagreements the more mysterious and the more disturbing in Kelly's memory for being wordless.

Don't ask. Sit up straight. It's fine. It's all right. You know you're someone's little girl don't you?

They would have a late dinner at the motel. Room service—of course. Impossible to risk the dining room. Any restaurant in Boothbay Harbor at the height of the tourist season.

She was not apprehensive, and she did not think, when the time came, she would be frightened. But she was alert. Sober. Memorizing the adventure.

How the headlights in wild drunken swings

illuminated the road that was scarcely wide enough for a single car and illuminated with a beauty that made her stare the swamp water in sheets outspread for miles on every side like bright shards of mirror amid the tangled vegetation.

At dusk, inland, darkness rose from the earth even as the sky retained light. There was a pale-glowering moon flat as a coin. Dyed-looking shreds of reddened cloud in the western sky and in the east at the ocean's horizon a sky shading subtly to night, bruised as an overripe plum.

Thinking, *Lost.*

Thinking, *An adventure.*

Thinking coolly even as her teeth rattled in her head as the man beside her braked the car, accelerated, braked, braked harder and accelerated harder, that she was not frightened, what she felt was excitement: that adrenaline-charge: as, on the beach, earlier that day, she'd felt the urgency of a man's desire, and vowed to herself, No I will *not.*

Even as that sly tickle of a thought ran through her head, Yes *why* not?

Poor Scorpio. Cunning Scorpio.

Thinking of how it had been chance, this Fourth of July on Grayling Island. She'd had other invitations. She hadn't been desperate for invitations for the long weekend. But she had decided to accept Buffy's invitation, and now she was here, now she was *here*, seated close beside The Senator on this wild wild ride to the ferry at Brockden's Landing, unsure where *here* was as night came on.

You're an American girl, you deserve to make YOUR wishes known and to have YOUR own way once in a while.

Just before the car flew off the road Kelly Kelleher wrinkled her nose smelling ... was it raw sewage?

Just before the car flew off the road Kelly Kelleher saw that she was gripping the strap at her shoulder so hard, her knuckles had gone white.

Just before the car flew off the road Kelly Kelleher at last said, as tactfully as possible, raising her voice without seeming to raise it—for The Senator seemed slightly hard of hearing in his right ear, "I think we're lost, Senator."

As a little girl Kelly had once spoken loudly to an uncle of hers when the family was seated at Thanksgiving dinner, and though Uncle Babcock was forever asking others to repeat themselves, and was forever complaining of people mumbling, he'd taken offense at Kelly's raised voice. Staring coldly at her saying, "Miss, you don't need to shout: *I'm* not deaf."

So too perhaps she had offended The Senator, who did not reply, sipping clumsily from his plastic cup and wiping his mouth on the back of his sunburnt hand and peering straight ahead, as if, unlike Kelly Kelleher, he could see through the shadowy swamp-thicket to the ocean that could not possibly be more than a few miles away.

And then The Senator said, a chuckle deep in his throat like phlegm, "This is a shortcut, Kelly. There's only one direction and we can't be lost."

"Yes," said Kelly, very carefully very tactfully, licking her lips which were parched, staring ahead too but seeing nothing except the headlights illuminating the tunnel of road, vegetation, mirror-shards glittering out of the shadows, "—but the road is so poor."

"Because it's a shortcut, Kelly. I'm sure."

Kelly!—her heart tripped absurdly, her face went hot, hearing her name, that name given her by schoolgirl friends, on this man's lips. So casually so intimately on this man's lips *as if he knows me, feels affection for me.*

Just before the car flew off the road.

8

KELLY: A NAME THAT SUITS YOU.

Yes? Why?—her hair whipping in the wind.

Green eyes?—they *are* green aren't they?

How tall he was, how physical his presence. And that dimpled grin, the big chunky white teeth. He made a playful swipe at lifting Kelly Kelleher's dark sunglasses to squint at her eyes and, adroitly, Kelly fell in with the gesture lifting the glasses herself meeting his frank examining gaze (blue: the blue of washed glass) but only for a moment.

And his grin wavered, just perceptibly. As

if, for that moment, he was doubting himself: his manly power.

Murmuring, as if in apology, even as, by so doing, he was flattering Kelly the more, Yes, green—*lovely*.

In fact Kelly Kelleher's eyes were rather more gray than green: pebble-colored, she thought them. Of no distinction except they were wide-spaced, large, attractive, "normal." But the lashes so pale, brittle, thin. Unless she used mascara, which she disliked, the lashes were scarcely visible.

In fact Kelly Kelleher's eyes had once been a source of great vexation and anguish to her parents, thus to her. Until the operation when things were set right.

From birth, Kelly had had an imbalance in her eye muscles, the name for the defect (you could not escape the fact, it *was* a defect) *strabismus*, meaning that, in Kelly's case, the muscles of the left were weaker than the muscles of the right. Unknowing, then, the child had been seeing for the first two confused years of her life not a single image registered in her brain as normal people do but two images (each further confused by a multiplicity of details) unharmoniously and always unpredictably overlapping, the left-eye image often floating about, un-

moored; so instinctively the child compensated
by focusing upon the stronger right-eye image,
thus the left eye wandered the more like a min-
now in the eyeball until it seemed (to the anxious elder Kellehers, Artie and Madelyn poor
Daddy and Mommy peering into their baby's
eyes repeatedly for the first twenty-four months
of her life, waggling fingers in front of her nose
asking questions trying to keep the worry, the
alarm, at times the impatience out of their
voices—poor Daddy especially for "abnormali-
ties" really upset him, no doubt it was a family
trait, laughingly defensively acknowledged: an
emphasis upon physical health, physical well-
being and attractiveness, *normality*) that Kelly
was impishly and stubbornly gazing at all times
to the left, over your head, beyond your range
of vision, even as, with her "good" right eye she
was looking you direct in the face as requested.

One of the doctors said exercise, a strict
regimen, another of the doctors said an operation as soon as possible, in some cases the child
doesn't outgrow it and in the interim the
weaker eye may become permanently atro-
phied, and Mommy and Grandma Ross (Mommy's mommy) wanted the exercises, give the
exercises a chance, and there was a nice thera-
pist, a young woman, wearing eyeglasses herself
optimistic about correcting Kelly's problem but
weeks passed, months, Daddy could scarcely

bear to look at his darling little girl sometimes, he loved her so, wanted to spare her hurt, harm, any sort of discomfort, and what irony, Artie Kelleher complained, laughing, angry, throwing his arms open wide as if to invite, as in a TV program the talk-show host so invites, an audience of anonymous millions to share in his bemusement, yes in his resentment too, his bafflement—what irony, things are going boom! boom! boom! in my business, like riding an escalator to the top floor, expansive-economy times these early years of the 1960s in building, construction, investments, you name it it's going up, what irony, my business life is absolutely great and my private life, my life-at-home—*I can't control*!

Speaking reasonably trying not to raise his voice (for, sometimes, Kelly was within earshot) so Mommy tried to respond in the same way though her voice trembling, hands trembling, you would not notice perhaps except for the beauty of her hands and her rings: the diamond cluster, the jade in its antique gold setting: as Daddy pointed out he was simply looking ahead, suppose the exercises don't work, it certainly doesn't seem that the exercises are working does it, all right use your imagination Madelyn look ahead to when she goes to school, you know damned well the other kids will tease her, they'll think she's a freak or something, do *you*

want that? is that what *you* want? so Mommy
burst into tears, No! no! of course not! no! why
do you say such things to me!

So one day, it was a weekday but Artie Kelleher took the morning off, the elder Kellehers
drove their little girl into the city, a forty-minute
trip from the suburban village of Gowanda
Heights, Westchester County, New York, and
there in Beth Israel Hospital on leafy East End
Avenue, there, at last, Elizabeth Anne Kelleher's
"bad" eye was corrected by surgery, and recov-
ery was swift, if not precisely painless as promised; and forever afterward the eye, the eyes, the
girl, were, as all outer signs indicated, normal.

9

"—LOST, SENATOR? THIS ROAD IS SO—"

"I said don't worry, Kelly!"—a sidelong glance, a tight smile puckering the corners of blood-veined eyes—"we'll get there, and we'll get there on time."

As liquid sloshed over the rim of the plastic cup and onto Kelly Kelleher's leg before she could prevent it.

The Senator had been among the three leading candidates for the Democratic presidential nomination in 1988; out of political prudence he had withdrawn his name, released his

delegates in favor of his old friend the Massachusetts governor.

In turn, Dukakis had asked The Senator to
be his running mate on the Democratic ticket.
The Senator had politely declined.

Of course, there was always the next presidential election, even the election beyond
that. The Senator, no longer young, was certainly not old: eleven years younger than
George Bush.

A man in the prime of his career—you
might say.

Kelly Kelleher envisioned herself working
for The Senator's presidential campaign. First,
though, she would work for his nomination at
the Democratic national convention. In the intimacy of the bouncing Toyota, her senses glazed
by the day's excitement, it was possible for
Kelly Kelleher, who rarely indulged in fantasies,
to give herself up to this one.

The evening before, as if anticipating this
adventure, Kelly had taken time, when so rarely
she took time, to file and polish her fingernails.
A pale pink-coral-bronze. Subdued, tasteful. To
match her lipstick.

"There's only one direction," The Senator
was saying, smiling, with the air of one deliv-
ering a self-evident truth, "—on an island."

Kelly laughed. Not knowing exactly why.

■   ■   ■

They were new acquaintances despite their intimacy in the speeding car. Virtual strangers despite the stealth with which they'd slipped away together.

So Kelly Kelleher had no name to call the driver of the Toyota, no name that sprang naturally and spontaneously to her lips as the black water flooded over the crumpled hood of the car, washed over the cracked windshield, over the roof, a sudden profound *darkening* as if the swamp had lurched up to claim them.

And the radio was out at once. The music to which neither had been listening was gone as if it had never been.

New acquaintances since approximately two o'clock that afternoon. By chance meeting at the oceanfront cottage on Derry Road, property of Mr. and Mrs. Edgar St. John of Old Lyme, Connecticut, who were not at the cottage at the time of the party; the hostess was Kelly's friend Buffy St. John with whom she'd roomed at Brown—Buffy, Kelly's closest friend.

Like Kelly Kelleher, Buffy St. John was twenty-six years old, and she too worked for a magazine published in Boston; but the magazine for which Buffy worked, *Boston After Hours*, was significantly different from the magazine for which Kelly worked, *Citizens' Inquiry*; and it might be said that Buffy was the more worldly of the two young women, the more experienced, the more "adventurous." Buffy painted her nails, finger- and toenails both, arresting shades of green, blue, and purple; and the condoms she carried in her several purses were frequently replenished.

Vehemently, as if her own integrity had been challenged, Buffy St. John would deny speculation that The Senator, a married man, and Kelly Kelleher had been lovers at the time of the accident; or even, before that day, acquaintances. Buffy would swear to it, Ray Annick would swear to it, The Senator and Kelly Kelleher had only just met that day, at the Fourth of July gathering.

Not lovers. Not friends, really. Simply new acquaintances who seemed, judging by the evidence, to have taken to each other.

As others who knew Kelly Kelleher would vehemently insist: she and The Senator had not known each other before that day for of course Kelly would have told us.

Kelly Kelleher wasn't the kind of young woman to be deceptive. To cultivate secrets.

We know her, we knew her. *She simply was not the type.*

So they were new acquaintances, which is very close to being strangers.

You would not choose to drown, to die, in such a way, trapped together in a sinking car, with a stranger.

Neither were they professionally associated, though it might be said that they shared certain political beliefs, liberal passions. Kelly Kelleher was not employed in any way nor had she ever been so employed by The Senator, his staff, his campaign organizers. It was true, certainly, she'd worked since graduation from college for an old acquaintance of The Senator's, a former political associate from the 1960s, Bobby Kennedy's whirlwind campaign, heady nostalgic days of power, purpose, authority, hope, youth in the Democratic Party—when, disastrous as things were, in Vietnam, at home, you did not expect them to worsen.

Kelly Kelleher had been not quite four years old at the time of Bobby Kennedy's assassination in June 1968. In all frankness, she remembered nothing of the tragedy. In any case her employer Carl Spader had a saying: *You're in politics, you're an optimist.*

You're no longer an optimist, you're no longer in politics.

You're no longer an optimist, you're dead.

In fact they had listened briefly to the car radio, at the very start of the drive, on bumpy Derry Road turning onto Post Road (a two-lane black-top highway, one of the Island's few paved roads) and there came suddenly on Kelly's right a badly weathered signpost listing a half-dozen place-names which Kelly had not been able to see distinctly, nor had The Senator, though between them there was the vague impression—

BROCKDEN'S LANDING 3.5 mi.

—at the same time The Senator, in high spirits, was whistling happily through his teeth, big perfect capped white teeth, saying, sighing, with sentimental pleasure, "God! that really takes me back!"—as, on the radio, out of speakers in the backseat of the car though somewhat muffled by the roar of the air conditioner which The Senator had turned on full blast as soon as he'd turned the keys in the ignition, there came a plaintive adenoidal instrumental version of a song not immediately familiar to Kelly Kelleher.

Not reproachfully so much as teasingly The Senator said, with a nudge of Kelly's arm, "Don't suppose you even know it, eh?"

Kelly listened. She would have liked to turn the frantic air conditioner down a notch but hesitated, for this was The Senator's car after all, and she his passenger. One thing Artie Kelleher did not appreciate was a passenger fiddling with his dashboard as he drove.

Cautiously Kelly Kelleher said, "Yes, I think I do. Except I can't remember the title."

"An old Beatles song—'All the Lonely People.'"

"Oh," said Kelly, nodding happily, "—yes."

Except this version had no words, this was New Age music. Synthesizers, echo chambers. Music like toothpaste squeezed very slowly from a tube.

"But I bet you're not a Beatles person, eh?" The Senator said, in that same teasing voice, "—too young," not a query so much as a statement, as, Kelly had noticed, The Senator was in the habit of making queries that were in fact statements, his mind shifting to the next subject, as, indeed, a new subject presented itself now, "Here's our turn!" braking the Toyota and turning the wheel sharply without having had time to signal so, close behind them, an angered motorist sounded his horn, but The Senator took no heed: not out of arrogance or hauteur but, simply, because he took no heed.

The badly rutted sandy road back into the marshes was known locally as Old Ferry Road though there was no longer any sign to designate it—there had been no sign for years.

Strictly speaking, The Senator was not lost at the time of the accident: he was headed in the right direction for Brockden's Landing, though, unknowingly, he had taken a road never used any longer since a new, paved Ferry Road existed, and the turn for this road was three-quarters of a mile beyond the turn for the old.

At about the time he'd finished his drink, and Kelly Kelleher gave him the one she'd been carrying for him: for the road.

They were new acquaintances, virtual strangers. Yet, what immediate rapport!

You know how it is, basking in the glow of a sudden recognition, his eyes, your eyes, an ease like slipping into warm water, there's the flawlessly beautiful woman who lies languorously sprawled as in a bed, long wavy red hair rippling out sensuously about her, perfect skin, heartbreak skin, lovely red mouth and a gown of some sumptuous gold lamé material clinging to breasts, belly, pubic area subtly defined by shimmering folds in the cloth, and The Lover stands erect and poised above her gazing down upon her his handsome darkish face not fully in focus, as the woman gazes up at him not required to smile in invitation, for she herself *is* the invitation, naked beneath the gold lamé gown, naked lifting her slender hips so subtly toward him, just the hint of it really, just the dream-suggestion of it really, otherwise the advertisement would be vulgar really, the perfume in its glittering bottle is OPIUM the perfume is OPIUM is OPIUM the *parfum* is OPIUM it will drive you mad it will drive him mad it will make addicts of you it is for sale in these stores ...

■   ■   ■

And, on their hike through the dunes, the wind whipping Kelly's hair, the gulls' wings flashing white above them, the beat beat beat of the surf like a pulsing in the loins, how assured his fingers gripping her bare shoulders, how shy yet eager her response: thinking *This can't be happening!* even as she was thinking *Something is going to happen that cannot be stopped.*

10

... THE THIN RED NEEDLE JOLTING UP BEYOND 40
mph as the Toyota hit a sandy rut and began to
skid like an explosively expelled sigh and The
Senator braked hard and quick exclaiming under
his breath and the skid continued as if with
more momentum, more purpose, as if the very
application of the brakes aroused willful resis-
tance in the vehicle that had seemed until now
so obedient, such a sort of plaything, a wild wild
roller coaster ride provoking that thrill deep in
the groin, and then, how had it happened, the
car was off the road, the car was skidding sideways off the road, the right rear wheel sliding

forward and the left front wheel back, the guardrail no sooner flew up out of the shadows than
it collapsed into pieces and there were seven-
foot broom-headed rushes slapping and scolding
at the windows, there was a crack! a crack! a
spiderweb-crack! of glass and a rude jolting and
rocking as in an earthquake and then the car
was in water, you would suppose a shallow
creek, a ditch, you would not suppose the car
would sink beneath the surface sinking and not
floating as black water foamy and churning
rushed over the crumpled hood, the windshield,
the car roof now bent in sharply on the passenger's side, and the door, the passenger's door,
buckled in, the way on the beach one of the
young guys had squeezed an aluminum can of
Miller Lite but still she could not draw sufficient
breath to scream nor did she even have a name
to call him, a name that flew unbidden and spontaneous to her lips.

11

WHEN FIRST SHE'D MET THE SENATOR IN THE EARLY afternoon of the Fourth of July, introduced to him by Buffy's lover Ray Annick, who was a lawyer-friend of The Senator's and had gone to school with him at Andover, Kelly Kelleher had been guarded, rather reticent. Inwardly skeptical. Observing this famous man shaking hands as he was, vigorously, delightedly, with that breathless air of having rushed hundreds of miles expressly for this purpose: shaking hands with you, and you, and you: standing a little apart, thinking, *He's one of them, forever campaigning.*

In the subsequent hours, Kelly was to radically revise her opinion of The Senator.

It could not be said that in those six hours Kelly Kelleher had fallen in love with The Senator, nor could it be said that The Senator had fallen in love with her, for such matters are private and unknowable; and what the future may have brought (in contrast to what the events of that night did in fact bring) will forever remain unknowable.

Except: Kelly certainly revised her opinion.

Thinking how instructive, how purifying for the soul (smiling into a mirror in the bathroom of the guest room that was hers at Buffy's, would have been hers again for the night of the Fourth had she not decided so precipitously to accompany The Senator back to the mainland) to learn that you are fallible, to be proven wrong.

Even if it's a merely interior, private proof.

Even if the one you've so carelessly misjudged never knows.

"Kelly, is it?—Callie? *Kelly.*"

It *was* absurd, wasn't it, that her heart should trip like a young girl's, hearing her name on The Senator's lips, for Kelly Kelleher was a mature young woman who'd had many lovers.

Several lovers, in any case.

In any case, since graduating from Brown, one serious lover—of whom she never spoke.

(Why won't you talk about G——, Kelly's friends Buffy, Jane, Stacey asked, not meaning to be intrusive but generally concerned for Kelly, misinterpreting her silence for a broken heart, her cynicism about men for depression, or despondency; her angry refusal to answer their taped telephone calls and to keep to herself at certain times for *suicidal tendencies* of which they dared speak only to one another, never to Kelly herself.)

Yet The Senator was such a physical presence! Climbing out of the rented black Toyota loose-jointed and peppy as a kid, smiling, greeting them all as the murmur passed among them like wildfire *It's him—Jesus, is it really him?* A youthful ardor shone about him like an aura.

Ray Annick had invited The Senator out to Grayling Island and Buffy had told her guests carefully, *I* don't expect him really. I'm sure he won't come.

The man was more vibrant, more compelling, there was that tacky word *charismatic*, than his television appearances suggested. For one thing, he was a big man: six feet four inches tall, weighing perhaps two hundred fifteen pounds. He carried himself well for a man in his midfifties who had the fatty-muscled body of a former athlete, with an athlete's wariness on his feet; even when his weight was on his heels (in comfortable scuffed beige canvas crepe-soled shoes from L. L. Bean) there was that air of poise, of springy anticipation. And his broad handsome-battered face, the eyes so transparently blue, the nose just slightly venous but a straight nose, lapidary, like the jaws, the chin, the familiar profile.

Tugging at his necktie, loosening the collar of his long-sleeved white cotton shirt—"I see the party has started without me, eh?"

He turned out to be really warm, really nice, not at all condescending, Kelly Kelleher began to compose her account of that memorable Fourth of July on Grayling Island—*spoke to us all as if we were, not just equals, but old friends.*

He'd kissed her, too. But that was later.

12

KELLY KELLEHER KNEW ABOUT POLITICIANS, SHE WAS
no fool. And not just from studying American
history and politics at Brown.

Her father, Arthur Kelleher, was a close
friend from school days and a golfing partner
of many years of Hamlin Hunt the Republican
congressman, and even when business was not
going well for Mr. Kelleher (as, since the stock
market debacle of a few years ago, it did not
seem to be going spectacularly well) he contrib-
uted to "Ham" Hunt's campaigns, helped host
immense fund-raising benefit dinners at the Gowanda Heights Country Club, took a childlike

pride in being included in Republican Party events local and statewide. The congressman, whom Kelly had known since elementary school, had lately become a controversial "colorful" figure with a national profile, he appeared frequently on television talk shows, was often interviewed on the news, as a maverick sort of conservative who spoke out derisively against every aspect of liberalism *except* abortion ... regarding abortion, Ham Hunt declared himself "pro-choice."

(In private, Hunt believed sincerely that the key to America's future salvation was abortion, abortion in the right demographic quarters, blacks, Hispanics, welfare mothers who start procreating with the onset of adolescence, something had to be done, something surely had to be done, abortion was the answer, the way to control the population which the white majority had better underwrite before it was too late—"And I know what I'm talking about, I've seen Calcutta, Mexico City. I've seen the townships in South Africa.")

Once, Kelly screamed at her astonished father, "How can you vote for such a man!—a fascist!—a Nazi!—he believes in genocide for Christ's sake!" and Mr. Kelleher merely stared at her as if she had slapped him in the face.

"How can he, Mother?—how can *you*?" Kelly asked her mother at a quieter moment, and Mrs. Kelleher regarded her fierce young daughter with a shiver of pride, and took her hand, and said, calmly, "Kelly, dear, please: how do you presume to know how *I* vote?"

During the most recent presidential election Kelly had volunteered her services working for Governor Dukakis's doomed campaign. She had not known the campaign was doomed until the final weeks of the contest, each time she saw or heard George Bush it seemed self-evident to her that anyone who saw or heard him must naturally reject him, for how transparently hypocritical! how venal! how crass! how uninformed! how *evil*! his exploitation of whites' fears of blacks, his CIA affiliation! his fraudulent piety! his shallow soul!—so too, until the final weeks, perhaps the final days, her coworkers at campaign headquarters (in Cambridge) had not seemed to understand that the Democratic campaign was doomed, though the national polls clearly indicated this, and the candidate Dukakis himself had a defiant rueful glassy-eyed air.

"Kelly, my God!—how could you!—wasting your time and energy on that asshole!"—so Artie Kelleher shouted over the phone.

When the votes came in, when the landslide was a fact, and the unthinkable became, simply, history, as so much that seems unthinkable becomes, simply, history, thus thinkable, Kelly had virtually stopped eating; had not slept for several nights in succession; felt a despair so profound and seemingly impersonal that she walked in the streets and eventually in Boston Common disheveled, dazed, vaguely smiling faint with hunger and nausea staring at, not human figures, but misshapen things, animal, fleshy, upright, clothed ... until she broke down crying, and fled, and telephoned her mother to plead please come get me, I don't know where I am.

13

SHE WAS THE GIRL, SHE WAS THE ONE HE'D CHOSEN, she was the one to whom it would happen, the passenger in the rented Toyota.

She was clawing at something that held her tight as an embrace as the black water churned and bubbled rising about her splashing into her eyes as she managed now to scream, drew breath to scream coughing and spitting screaming at last as the Toyota sank on its side on the passenger's side in murky churning water.

Her baptismal name was "Elizabeth Anne Kelleher." And, on the masthead of *Citizens' Inquiry: A Bi-Weekly Publication of the Citizens'*

Inquiry Foundation, the name was "Elizabeth Anne Kelleher."

Known to her friends as "Kelly."

An immediate warm rapport between them, you know how it happens sometimes. Unexpectedly.

As he'd smiled happily gripping her hand squeezing it just perceptibly too hard unconsciously as men sometimes do, as some men sometimes do, needing to *see* to *feel* that pin-prick of startled pain in your eyes, the contraction of the pupil.

As G——, making love, had sometimes hurt her. Unconsciously.

She'd cried out, short high-pitched gasping cries, she'd sobbed, she'd heard her voice distant, wild, pleading reverberating out of the corners of the darkened room, Oh I love you, I love you, I love love love you, their bodies slapping and sucking hot-clammy with sweat, hair plastered to their heads with sweat, *you know you're somebody's little girl don't you? don't you?*

His weight on her, and his arms around her, her legs tight-quivering around his hips, then her trembling knees drawn up awkwardly to her shoulders so he could go deepest in her, Yes! yes! like that! oh Christ! and she knew that G——'s lips were drawn back from his teeth in that grimace, that death's-head triumph, that excluded her.

.   .   .

Very near the end he'd said quietly, "I don't
want to hurt you, Kelly, I hope you know that,"
and Kelly smiled saying, "Yes, I know that," as
if this were a casual conversation, one of their
easy friendly conversations, for weren't they
more than lovers, weren't they best friends too,
she'd kissed him, he'd slung an arm around her
burying his warm face in her neck, she was very
still thinking, And can't I hurt you? Have I not
that power, to hurt *you*? Knowing that she did
not have it, any longer.

The winter afternoon waned. Shadows rose
out of the corners of the room, it became a
room Kelly did not know. G—— nudged his
head against hers, and said, "I knew you knew.
But I wanted to make sure."

And now what held her tight?—a band?—several bands?—across her chest and thighs, her
left arm tangled in one of them?—and her
forehead had cracked hard against something
she hadn't seen, it was pitch-black she was
blinking squinting trying to see, she was
blind and that roaring in her ears as of a
jet plane and a man's voice incredulous "Oh
God. Oh God. Oh God."

She was the girl, she was the one, she was
the passenger, she was the one trapped in the
safety belts, no it was the door and part of the

roof that had buckled in upon her, she was upside down was she? thrown on her right side
was she? and where was up? and where was the
top? and where was the air? the weight of his
body thrown upon her too struggling and gasping for air pleading "Oh God" a sob in his voice,
a man's voice, a stranger's voice, you would not
choose to die like this, to drown, in murky black
water with a stranger, but her right leg was
pinned, as in a clamp, her right kneecap had
been crushed but she had no sensation of pain,
she might have been in shock, she might have
been dead, so soon! so soon! the black water
filling her lungs to drown her lungs thus the
oxygen to her brain would cease thus her
thoughts would cease and yet her thoughts
were detached and even logical: *This isn't
happening.*

This person, this man, his weight thrown
on top of her—she'd forgotten who it was. He
too clawing and clutching and scrambling and
kicking frantic to get out of the capsized car.

That distinct voice, a stranger's—"Oh God."

Not in a curse but in a hortatory appeal.

Had the speeding Toyota not lost control
on the hairpin curve estimating a probable
speed of forty-five miles an hour from the skid
marks in the road and the considerable degree
of damage to the vehicle it would very likely
have collided with the railing of the narrow

bridge ahead with a subsequent crash, a fall into the water, a similar result. Or so it would be speculated.

The name of the fast-running stream was Indian Creek. You would not have thought it had a name. In the marshy wasteland, in the seemingly uncharted swamp dense with mosquitoes and shrill with nocturnal insects in a midsummer frenzy of procreation.

You would not have expected a creek, as deep as eleven feet in some stretches, twenty feet wide, running in a northeasterly direction to empty into a tidal pool of the Atlantic Ocean, thus into the ocean, approximatley two miles to the east in Brockden's Landing.

Am I going to die? Like this?

And no witnesses. And no other motorists traveling on Old Ferry.

As if to punish her for her behavior her performance as *a self not herself: not Kelly Kelleher really* but she rejected such a thought, she was not superstitious, she did not believe in even the Anglican God.

He had chosen her. You could see that from the first. The quick rapport! the ease of their smiles! a girl his daughter's age!

Yes they had surprised the others—a few of the others. Those who knew. Disappointing Buffy St. John by saying they were leaving to catch the 8:20 P.M. ferry to Boothbay Harbor.

Actually, as Buffy would recall, The Senator had wanted to catch an earlier ferry ... but, somehow, they hadn't left on time ... The Senator had another drink. Or two.

The Senator and Kelly Kelleher his passenger had left the party at 17 Derry Road at approximately 7:55 P.M. Which gave them twenty-five minutes to get to the ferry, enough time if you drive fast and if you take the right route.

Turning onto Old Ferry was the mistake but it was an understandable mistake, you would not need to be *under the influence of alcohol* to make such a mistake at dusk.

Old Ferry, no longer maintained by Grayling Township, should have been officially shut down: ROAD OUT.

Three hundred acres of the swampland were preserved as the Grayling Island Wildlife Sanctuary under a federal funding. Such birds as phalaropes, whippoorwills, swifts, both surface-feeding and diving ducks, egrets, great blue herons, terns, killdeers, many varieties of woodpeckers, thrushes, tanagers, as well as the more common of northeastern birds. Such marsh vegetation as cattails, sea oats, sedge, wool grass, pickerelweed, dozens of varieties of rushes and reeds, jack-in-the-pulpit, trillium, marsh marigold, arrowhead, water arum. Such animals as ... Kelly Kelleher had in fact skimmed a tourist flyer at Buffy's cottage, she'd read about the

wildlife sanctuary a few miles away, yes Buffy
had gone of course many times when she was
a kid and the family spent summers out here
but she had not gone in recent years and maybe
next day if Ray was in the mood they could
drive over it *was* a beautiful place unless they
all had hangovers unless Ray had other plans
unless it was just too hot but Kelly was thinking
yes she'd go by herself preferably, she'd make a
point of going, borrow someone's car or maybe
if it wasn't too far Buffy's bicycle: a brand-new
mountain bike.

Have you ever ridden one of these before?—no? Try it.

Gripping the handguards, her feet on the
pedals, rising, standing at first, spine arched, but-
tocks arched, long coppery hair whipping in the
wind, smiling at the childish pleasure of hurtling
herself along the beach, the bicycle's thick
ridged tires biting into the crusty sand, what
quick speed, what happiness, little Lizzie flying
as Mommy, Daddy, Grandma and Grandpa watch,
Oh be careful honey! careful! but she'd laughed
flying out of the range of their eyes, their voices.

Now, at Buffy's, in her new swimsuit fitting
her slender body like a glove, white spandex,
teasing little pearl buttons, a single strap, the
invisible underwire bra lifting her breasts pushing them together so there was a shadowy cleav-
age and she'd seen his eyes drop there

unconsciously, she'd seen his casual gaze take
in her ankles her legs her thighs her breasts her
shoulders bare except she'd slipped on a
daffodil-yellow crocheted tunic out of modesty
perhaps out of her old shyness regarding her
body so unlike Buffy in her silky black bikini
her campy-lewd glitter-green fingernails and toenails, Buffy with her flawless skin, her funny
"faux" ponytail, brash enough and confident
enough to slap her thighs in Ray's presence crying Cellulite! that's what this is: cellulite! I'm
too fucking young for cellulite God damn it!

And they'd all laughed. *He'd* laughed.

Buffy St. John who was so beautiful. So confident in her oiled heated skin.

Since freshman year at Brown Kelly had had
the habit of starving herself to discipline herself
to maintain rigorous control to lighten her men-
strual periods and, after G——, to punish herself
for having loved a man more than the man
seemed to have loved her, but this past year she
was determined to be *healthy*, to be *normal*,
forcing herself to eat regularly and she'd regained eleven of the twenty pounds she'd lost,
she slept without sleeping pills not requiring
even the single glass of red wine she and G——
had made a ritual of before going to bed during
those three months G—— had actually lived
with her: not even that.

So she'd regained *health*, *normality*. She

was an American girl *you want to look your best and give your ALL.*

Yet avoiding the house in Gowanda Heights. Guilty of making her mother worry about her, guilty of provoking quarrels with her father, those "political" quarrels that were really about Daddy's authority unheeded, but relations between them were all right now and Kelly was fine now discreetly avoiding certain of her old friends the embittered idealists the angry pro-abortionists and even Mr. Spader after this most recent divorce (his third) unshaven, potbellied, losing his fiery hair, sixty-year-old babyface the dimpled smile grown dented, sodden, and she'd been acutely embarrassed that day in the office feeling his eyes on her, hearing his hoarse breath, there were hairs in his ears and nostrils like Brillo wire poor Carl Spader once a media personality an eloquent young white associate of Martin Luther King and John F. Kennedy and now the dismal storefront office on Brimmer Street and *Citizens' Inquiry* with its fluctuating circulation of 35,000–40,000 where at its peak in 1969 it had had a circulation of 95,000–100,000 rivaling *The New Republic* but never get Carl Spader going on the subject of *The New Republic*, where in fact he'd worked for several years after college! never get Carl Spader going on the subject of the triumph of conservatism in our time, the heartbreak, the tragedy, the dismantling of the Kennedy-Johnson vision, the loss of America's soul never get him started!— Kelly was discreet answering The Senator's questions about his old friend Spader, Kelly Kelleher was not one to gossip carelessly, nor was she one to exploit another's misfortune for meretricious conversational purposes, it was a principle of hers that you must never say anything about another person you would not say in that person's presence.

The Senator several times turned the conversation back to Carl Spader, whom he had not, he said, seen in years. In The Senator's voice there was a tone both regretful and mildly censorious.

Yes of course he read *Citizens' Inquiry*—certainly.

His office in Washington had a subscription. Of course.

He'd asked Kelly what she did for the magazine and Kelly told him mentioning her recent article "The Shame of Capital Punishment in America" and The Senator said why yes, yes he'd read that article, he believed he had read it, he'd been impressed.

As, on Buffy's great new bike, she'd felt his eyes follow her too.

Politics, the negotiating of power. Eros, the negotiating of power.

Gripping her shoulders bare beneath the

crocheted tunic with his strong fingers and kissing her full on the mouth as the wind blew caressingly about them like a palpable tactile substance wrapping them together, binding. He had kissed her suddenly yet not unexpectedly. Hiking in the dunes behind the St. Johns' house, the gulls flashing white overhead, their knifelike wings, deadly beaks, excited cries. The pounding splashing surf. Beat beat beat of the surf. She'd heard it the night before sleepless hearing muffled sounds of laughter, lovemaking from Buffy and Ray's room, underneath such human cries the beat of the surf, the rising of the tide, the moon's tide, a tide in her blood, the almost unbearable rush of the man's desire so it was understood between them that he would kiss her again and Kelly's seemingly impulsive decision to go with him to catch the ferry instead of spending the night of the Fourth at Buffy's as planned was a public acknowledgment of this fact.

She was the one, the one he'd chosen. The one in the speeding car. The passenger.

Scorpio don't be shy, poor silly Scorpio your stars are WILDLY romantic now. Demand YOUR wishes. YOUR desires for once.

So she did, she had and would. She *was* the one.

14

TASTING STILL THE BEERY WARMTH AND PRESSURE OF
The Senator's mouth on hers. The forceful probing tongue.

Even as the nameless road flew out from
under the Toyota she was tasting it. Smiling
wryly thinking how often in her life had kisses
tasted of beer, of wine, of alcohol, of tobacco,
of hash. The many probing tongues. *Am I ready?*

She'd been staring at the moon out of the
jolting car. How queerly flat-looking, how bright.
Lit from within you'd think and not mere re-
flected light you'd think but you'd be wrong for

thinking, reasoning, calculating out of your own brain is not enough: poor Scorpio.

Of course Kelly Kelleher did not believe in anything so idiotic as a horoscope, astrology. In her innermost heart though she was a volunteer for the National Literacy Foundation of America she felt a certain contempt for ignorant people, not just blacks of course (though all of her students were black) but whites, whatever: men and women whom the ruthless progress of civilization had left behind really, their limited intelligences could not grasp certain facts of life really, no doubt as Artie Kelleher and Ham Hunt and all of conservative America believed it *was* hopeless thus save your own white skin but Kelly Kelleher angrily rejected such selfishness, had she not committed in writing a shameful statement to her own parents composed on her word processor at college and carefully revised and signed with her baptismal name "Elizabeth Anne Keller" and mailed to the Kelleher home in Gowanda Heights, New York, in partial explanation of why she was not coming home for Thanksgiving this year but going to Old Lyme with her roommate, *I will always love you Mother and Father but I have come to realize I would not live the lives you live for anything, please forgive me!*

Kelly had been nineteen years old at the time.

The wonder of it was, her parents *had* forgiven her.

The Senator was of a social background similar to that of the Kellehers, he too had gone to Andover just after Arthur Kelleher had graduated, then he'd gone to Harvard for both his B.A. and his law degree and Arthur Kelleher had gone to Amherst and then to Columbia and very likely The Senator and the Kellehers knew many people in common but in their meandering disjointed excitable conversation that day neither The Senator nor Kelly Kelleher had chosen to pursue the subject.

She knew that The Senator had children her age—a son?—a son and a daughter?—but neither mentioned this of course.

She knew that The Senator was separated from his wife of approximately thirty years and this fact The Senator did mention, or allude to, very briefly.

Saying, with a smile, I'm alone this weekend: my wife's having her family out to our place on the Cape ... his voice trailing off inconclusively.

Tasting his mouth on hers. And earlier that day when Kelly had been sitting with her head resting on her arms at a picnic table apart from the others sleepy and sun-dazed and slightly ill (*why* did she drink? when it affected her so unpredictably? was it simply to be one of a party, as in college? was it simply to appear to be one of a party, as in college?) when someone came up steathily beside her, she saw through her eyelashes that the person was barefoot, a man, large white veined feet, gnarled-looking toenails, and there came the lightest most shimmering touch on her bare shoulder, a touch that ran through her like an electric shock as she realized it was his tongue on her skin ... his warm soft damp tongue on her bare skin.

Staring up then into his face. His eyes. The whites faintly yellowed as with fatigue, threaded with blood, but the irises startlingly blue. Like colored glass with nothing behind it.

And not a word passed between them for what seemed like a very long time though Kelly's lips twitched wanting to smile or make a nervous girlish joke to break the spell.

You know you're someone's little girl, oh yes!

Recalling this as they sped into the desolate area southeast of Brockden's Landing as dusk deepened and it began to look (to Kelly at least) that they would not make the 8:20 P.M. ferry.

The place was dense with mosquitoes and here and there fireflies and some of the blond broom-headed rushes grew to a grotesque height swaying top-heavy in the wind, like human figures grotesque without faces so she shivered seeing them. Remarking to The Senator it was strange wasn't it that so many of the trees in the marsh seemed to be dead ... *were* they dead? ... isolated tree trunks in the twilit gloom denuded of leaves, limbs, bark gray and shiny-smooth as old scar tissue.

"I hope it isn't pollution of some kind, killing the trees."

The Senator, hunched over the wheel, frowning, exerting pressure on the gas pedal, made no reply.

Had not spoken directly to her, Kelly was thinking, since they'd turned off onto this damned road.

Since G——, last June when it had finally ended, Kelly Kelleher had not made love with any man.

Since G——, when she had wanted to die, she had not touched any man in desire; nor even in the pretense of desire.

Am I ready? ready? ready?—a small mocking voice.

On all sides were shrill shrieking nocturnal insects in a frenzy of copulation, procreation. A din of cries, near-deafening—she shivered, hearing them. So many. You would not think that God would make so many. Their frenzied cries as if in the very heat of midsummer sensing the imminent and inevitable waning of the heat, the quickening of night, and cold, their tiny deaths flying at them out of the future and Kelly Kelleher swallowed hard regretting now she had not brought a drink along for herself thinking, *Am I ready?*

Like a mirror broken and scattered about them, the marshes stretching for miles. Kelly supposed they were lost but hesitated to utter the word for fear of annoying The Senator.

Am I ready?—it's an adventure.

In the jolting car they did seem immune to any harm, still less to a vehicular accident, for The Senator was driving in a way one might call recklessly, you might say his judgment was impaired by drink but not his skill as a driver for he *did* have skill, handling the compact car as if by instinct and with an air too of kingly contempt, so Kelly was thinking, though they were lost, though they would not make the 8:20 P.M. ferry after all, she was privileged to be here and no harm could come to her like a young princess in a fairy tale so recently begun but perhaps it would not end for some time, perhaps.

The bright flat moon, the glittering patches of water so very like pieces of mirror. A jazzy tempo to the radio music now and the beat, the beat, the beat of the surf out of range of their immediate hearing but Kelly believed she could hear it half-closing her eyes gripping the strap at her shoulder so hard her knuckles were white.

Raising her voice without seeming quite to raise it: "I think we're lost, Senator."

The word *Senator* lightly ironic, playful. A kind of caress.

He had told her to call him by his first name—his diminutive first name—of course. But somehow just yet Kelly had not been able to oblige.

Such intimacy, together in the bouncing jolting car. The giddy smell of alcohol pungent between them. Beery kisses, that tongue thick enough to choke you.

Here was one of the immune, beside her: *he*, one of the powerful adults of the world, manly man, U.S. senator, a famous face and a tangled history, empowered to not merely endure history but to guide it, control it, manipulate it to his own ends. He was an old-style liberal Democrat out of the 1960s, a Great Society man with a stubborn and zealous dedication to social reform seemingly not embittered or broken or even greatly surprised at the opposition his humanitarian ideas aroused in the America of the waning years of the twentieth century for his life was politics, you know what politics is, in its essence: the art of compromise.

Can compromise be an art?—yes, but a minor art.

Kelly had thought The Senator had not heard her but then he said, with a mirthless chuckle as if clearing his throat, "This is a short-cut, Kelly." As if speaking to a very young child or to a drunken young woman, slowly. "There's only one direction and we can't be lost."

Just before the car flew off the road.

15

SHE HEARD THE SINGLE EXPLETIVE "HEY!" AS THE CAR skidded into a guardrail skidding sideways, the right rear coming around as in a demonic amusement ride and her head cracked against the window a red mist flashing across her eyes but she could not draw breath to scream as the momentum of their speed carried them down a brief but steep embankment, an angry staccato tapping against the car as if dried sticks were being broken, still she had not breath to scream as the car plunged into what appeared to be a pit, a pool, stagnant water in the marshland you might think only a few feet deep but black water was churning alive and purposeful on all sides tugging them down, the car sinking on its side, and Kelly was blinded, The Senator fell against her and their heads knocked and how long it was the two of them struggled together, stunned, desperate, in terror of what was happening out of their control and even their comprehension except to think *This can't be happening, am I going to die like this,* how many seconds or minutes before The Senator moaning "Oh God. Oh God" fumbled clawing at the safety belts extricating himself by sheer strength from his seat behind the broken steering wheel and with fanatic strength forcing himself through the door, opening the door against the weight of black water and gravity that door so strangely where it should not have been, overhead, directly over their heads, as if the very earth had tilted insanely on its axis and the sky now invisible was lost in the black muck beneath—how long, in her terror and confusion Kelly Kelleher could not have said. She was fighting to escape the water, she was clutching at a man's muscular forearm even as he shoved her away, she was clutching at his trousered leg, his foot, his foot in its crepe-soled canvas shoe heavy and crushing upon her striking the side of her head, her left temple so now she did cry out in pain and hurt grabbing at his leg frantically, her fingernails tearing, then at his ankle, his foot, his shoe, the crepe-soled canvas shoe that came off in her hand so she was left behind crying, begging, "Don't leave me!—help me! Wait!"

Having no name to call him as the black water rushed upon her to fill her lungs.

PART
TWO

PART
1971

16

HE WAS GONE BUT WOULD COME BACK TO SAVE HER.

He was gone having swum to shore to cry
for help . . . or was he lying on the weedy embankment vomiting water in helpless spasms drawing
his breath deep, deep to summon his strength and
manly courage preparatory to returning to the
black water to dive down to the submerged car
like a capsized beetle helpless and precariously
balanced on its side in the soft muck of the river-
bed where his trapped and terrified passenger
waited for him to save her, waited for him to
return to open the door to pull her out to save
her: was that the way it would happen?

I'm here. I'm here. Here.

17

AT THE FOURTH OF JULY GATHERING AT BUFFY ST. John's that day there were guests arriving all afternoon and into the evening, some of whom Kelly Kelleher did not know but she did know and was known by Ray Annick and Felicia Ch'en a glossy-black-haired strikingly beautiful new friend of Buffy's who had a degree in mathematics and wrote freelance science articles for the *Boston Globe* and Ed Murphy the finance economist at B.U. who was a consultant for a Boston brokerage house and Stacey Miles of course who'd been a suitemate at Brown and Randy

Post the architect with whom Stacey lived in
Cambridge and there was an ex-lover of Buffy's
named Fritz with whom Buffy remained good
friends and who had in fact taken Kelly Kelleher
out a few times amicably, casually, he'd hoped
to make love to her Kelly had surmised as re-
venge of sorts upon Buffy who would not in any
case have cared in the slightest, and there was
that tall big-shouldered balding light-skinned
black man of about thirty-five a fellow of some
kind at M.I.T. whom Kelly had met before, his
first name was unusual, exotic, was it Lucius?—
a Trinidadian and not an American black and
Kelly remembered liking him and knew that he
liked her, was attracted to her, so Kelly felt good
about that, she had dreaded this weekend having become increasingly uncomfortable at parties like this where so much drinking so much
repartee so much gaiety so much frank sexual
appraisal put her at a disadvantage, she was vul-
nerable as if the outer layer of her skin had been
peeled away since G—— and if men looked at
her she stiffened feeling her jaws tighten her
blood beat with dread and if men did not look
at her, if their glances slipped past her as if she
were invisible, she felt a yet deeper dread: a
conviction of not merely female but human
failure.

But there was Lucius. A research fellow in

plasma physics. A subscriber to *Citizens' Inquiry* and an admirer of Carl Spader, or what he knew of Carl Spader.

There was Lucius, and Kelly was grateful for his presence, and had not shortly past two o'clock a black Toyota turned into Buffy's drive and the murmur went up *Is it him?—is it?— Jesus!* the two might have become, in time, very good friends.

18

SHE DID NOT BELIEVE IN ASTROLOGY, IN THE BREATH-
less admonitions and Ben Franklin-pep talks of
the magazine horoscopes, nor did she believe
in the Anglican God to Whom—in Whom?—for
Whom?—she had long ago been confirmed.

Grandpa Ross when he was dying his flesh
shriveling back from the bone but his eyes alert
as always, kindly brimming with love for her
whom he knew as, never "Kelly," but "Lizzie,"
his dearest grandchild of the several grandchil-
dren for whom he had been a conduit into the
world told her as if imparting a worrisome se-
cret, *The way you make your life, the love you
put into it—that's God.*

19

SHE WAS ALONE. HE HAD BEEN WITH HER, AND HE WAS gone and now she was alone but *he has gone to get help of course.*

In her shock not knowing at first where she was, what tight-clamped place this was, what darkness, not knowing what had happened because it had happened so abruptly like a scene blurred with speed glimpsed from a rushing window and there was blood in her eyes, her eyes were wide open staring and sightless, her head pounding violently where the bone was cracked, she knew the bone was cracked believing that it would be through this fissure the black water would pour to extinguish her life unless she could find a way to escape unless *he will be back to help me of course.*

In fact he was comforting her, smiling, frowning concerned and solicitous touching her shoulder with his fingertips. *Don't doubt me, Kelly. Never.*

He knew her name, he had called her by name. He had looked at her with love so she knew.

He was her friend. He was no one she knew but he was her friend, *that* she knew. In another minute she would remember his name.

It was a car that had trapped her, she was jammed somehow in the front seat of a car but the space was very small because the roof and the dashboard and the door beside her had buckled inward pinning her legs and crushing her right kneecap held as if in a vise and her ribs on that side were broken but the pain seemed to be held in suspension like a thought not yet fully acknowledged scarcely any sensation at all so she knew she would be all right so long as she could lift her head free of the seeping black water that smelled of raw sewage and was cold, colder than you could imagine on such a warm midsummer night.

She would manage to breathe even while swallowing water, there was a way to do it, snorting water out of her nose, thrashing her head from side to side then leaning as far as her strength would allow her away from the smashed door, her left shoulder was broken perhaps, she would not think of it now for in the hospital they would take care of her, they had saved her friend once, her friend from school the girl whose name she could not remember except to know that Kelly was not that girl, she was calling *Help, help me!—here—*confused because where was up? where was the sky?—he'd been desperate to get free using her very body to lever himself out the door overhead where no door should be, forcing the door open against the weight of whatever it was that pressed it down and squeezing his big-boned body through that space that seemed scarcely large enough for Kelly Kelleher herself to squeeze through but he was strong he was frantic kicking and scrambling like a great upright maddened fish knowing to save itself by instinct.

And what did she have of him, my God what prize did her silly fingers clutch, her broken nails she'd taken time to polish the night before, using Buffy's polish, what was it for God's sake—a shoe?

An empty shoe?

But no: there is only one direction, and he would come to her from that direction. She knew.

. . .

Except, she knew also that the car, submerged,
how many feet below the surface of the water
she couldn't guess, it might be only a few inches
in fact, with a part of her brain that remained
pragmatic, pitiless she knew that though the car
retained air, a bubble, or bubbles, of air, it
would fill by degrees, it could not not fill, thin
trickles of water pushing through myriad holes,
fissures, cracks like the webbed cracks in the
windshield, by degrees the water level would
rise, must rise, since the car was totally submerged, she'd heard of accident victims surviv-
ing in submerged cars for as many as five hours
and then rescued and she would be rescued if
she was patient if she did not panic but by degrees the filthy black water would rise to fill her
mouth, her throat, her lungs though she could
not see it nor could she hear it trickling, seeping, draining beyond the blow to her head, the
roaring in her ears, spasms of coughing and
choking that seized her, black muck to be spat
up.

Except had he not promised her?—he had.

Except had he not held her, kissed her?—
he had.

Penetrated her dry, alarmed mouth with his
enormous tongue?—he had.

No pain! no pain! she swore she felt no
pain, she would give in to no pain, they'd

praised her so brave 'Lizabeth, brave little girl when her eye had been bandaged and that was her truest self, he would see, as soon as he helped her free she would save herself, she was a strong swimmer. *I'm here.*

20

TWICE WEEKLY, TUESDAYS AND THURSDAYS EVEN IN summer, Kelly Kelleher made the arduous drive in her secondhand Mazda from her condominium up behind Beacon Hill, Boston, out to Roxbury, where in an ill-ventilated community services center she taught, or made the spirited effort of teaching, black adult illiterates to read primer texts. Her classes began at 7 P.M. and ended, sometimes trailed ambiguously off, at 8:30 P.M. Asked what progress she and her several students were making Kelly would say, with a smile, "Some!"

Kelly was a volunteer of only a few months

in the National Literacy Foundation of America
program and she felt both enthusiasm and zeal
for what she did . . . yet a priggish self-righteous-
ness too, a Caucasian condescension mingled
with a very real and visceral fear of physical
threat, harm, not within the community services
center itself but in the streets surrounding, in
desolate Roxbury and along the debris-strewn
expressway, in the vulnerability of her white
skin.

This ambivalence so qualified her experi-
ence in Roxbury that she had yet to tell her
parents about it by midsummer, and rarely mentioned it to her friends.

Nor did she mention it to The Senator during their several conversations that day at Buffy's . . . not knowing why, exactly . . . perhaps
hoping to seem, not the zealous *volunteer type*
with whom The Senator like any successful politician was contemptuously familiar, but another
type altogether.

What's a volunteer, especially a lady volunteer?
Someone who knows she can't sell it.

As the black water drained into the space that
contained her snug as any womb.

Except: Buffy had been sweet giving her the
little-sister's room as they called it, the south-

east-corner room of the five-bedroom Cape Cod
on Derry Road, how many times had Kelly Kelleher been a guest there, a room with a chaste
white-organdy brass bed and spare Shaker-in-
spired furniture and braided rugs and that floral
wallpaper predominantly the hue of strawberries so like Grandma Ross's favorite room in the
big old house in Greenwich, and with trembling
fingers Kelly had washed her warm face, took
time to rinse her sun-dazed eyes, brushed her
hair in swift brisk excited strokes smiling at herself in the bathroom mirror thinking, *It's wild,
it can't happen.*

But, yes. Kelly Kelleher was the one.

At first The Senator was speaking generally, to
everyone. Tall and broad-shouldered and vehe-
ment and ruddy with pleasure at being where
he was, this place, beautiful Grayling Island of
which he'd known virtually nothing, he'd visited
Maine infrequently since they summered on the
Cape mainly, his family place on the Cape, bent
upon ignoring how the Cape had changed over
the years, so developed, overpopulated ...
"Some facts of life, things closest around you,
you sometimes don't want to *see*."

But The Senator's tone was expansive, gregarious. This was a happy occasion, an attractive, younger crowd, he had the air of a man
determined to enjoy himself.

He and Ray Annick: the two older men, you might say: determined to enjoy themselves.

Actually, the first thing The Senator did after greeting his hostess was to draw Ray Annick off to confer with him, out of earshot of the others; then he asked Buffy could he freshen up, use Ray's shaving kit—he hadn't shaved, he said, since six o'clock that morning in Washington.

He changed out of his inappropriately formal white cotton long-sleeved shirt into a short-sleeved navy blue polo shirt open at the collar, the knit sleeves tight on his fleshy biceps. In the shallow V of the collar, a bristle of steely-gray hairs.

He was wearing pale seersucker trousers. That crisp summery puckered look.

And beige canvas crepe-soled sporty shoes, L. L. Bean.

So there were drinks, on the breezy terrace, many voices simultaneously, and The Senator easy, friendly, unself-conscious among them though his posture and a certain focusing of speech, a moderation of tone suggested *I realize you are memorizing me, but don't for that reason dislike me* as they spoke of the outrage of the recent Supreme Court decisions, the ideologically sanctioned selfishness and cruelty of a wealthy society, how systematic the dismantling of the gains of the civil rights movement, the retirement of Justice Thurgood Marshall, the end of an era.

The Senator sighed, grimaced, seemed about to say something further, but changed his mind.

At Buffy's, always there were distractions. New guests arriving, the prospect of an impromptu tennis tournament.

Shaking Kelly Kelleher's small-boned hand, squeezing. "Kelly, is it? Callie? *Kelly.*"

She'd laughed. Liking the sound of her schoolgirl name on a U.S. senator's lips.

He wasn't as I'd imagined him, he turned out to be really warm, really nice, not at all condescending—

Shaping the precise words that would encapsulate, in her memory, in her recounting of memory to friends, perhaps Mr. Spader himself who had known The Senator years ago but was distant from him now.

How courteous, genuinely friendly, interested in who we were and what we thought of his Senate proposals, the Medicaid, the welfare reform, yes and he is a visionary, I don't think it is an exaggeration to say—

How crucial for us to rehearse the future, in words.

Never to doubt that you will live to utter them.

Never to doubt that you will tell *your story.*

And the accident too, one day she would transform the accident, the nightmare of being trapped in a submerged car, the near-drowning, the rescue. *It was horrible—hideous. I was trapped and the water was seeping in and he'd gone for help and fortunately there was air in the car, we'd had the windows shut tight, the air conditioner on, yes I know it's a miracle if you believe in miracles.*

21

ACNE CAN OCCUR AT ANY TIME NOT JUST ADOLESCENCE! Extra cells are produced in the skin pore lining, which blocks the exit of oils causing oil and bacteria to build up behind the plug. This leads then to whiteheads and blackheads and in cases of severe acne cyst formations. Recommended use of BENZOYL PEROXIDE an antibacterial medication and SALICYLIC ACID to cleanse and clear affected pores. Recommended green-tinted cosmetic underbase to neutralize the reddened skin areas then cover with sheer light-weight foundation and face powder.

NEVER apply foundation directly to open acne lesion for this can result in infection!

I want him to. His eyes, his hands. His mouth . . . Must stop staring.

Her hair, her eyes, her lips . . . What is that fragrance?

White spandex swimsuit with tiny pearl buttons for that lingerie look. Single shoulder strap and cut HIGH on the thighs so you will want to be golden tan ALL OVER.

Daffodil-yellow cotton mesh tunic to be worn all summer with chiffon, jeans, swimwear: smart, versatile, and SEXY.

CAUTION: the sun's ultraviolet rays, saltwater swimming, and overheated blow dryers are serious dangers to BEAUTIFUL HAIR.

CAUTION: More than 100,000 American women are infected with the AIDS virus.

CAUTION: Beware of disreputable modeling schools promising fashion magazine assignments within twelve months.

CAUTION: Perfume, hair spray, and mousse that contain alcohol can cause permanent damage to silk and acetate garments. Spray *before* dressing or place a towel over shoulders before you spray.

∎   ∎   ∎

SCORPIO'S MYSTERY. Pluto, God of the Under-
world, was originally NOT a man but a woman—
daughter of the Earth Mother Rhea. Pluto is but
a masculinized goddess! It is believed that with
the dawning of the New Age long-suppressed
Scorpio powers will be rediscovered and the
Scorpion will evolve to a new level—the PHOE-
NIX RESURRECTED.

22

SHE WAS NOT SCREAMING NOW NOR WAS SHE SOBBING knowing that the oxygen in this darkness must not be depleted but she spoke loudly and clearly her throat raw *I'm here I'm here I'M HERE*.

She was not hysterical. She was not paralyzed with terror.

She could hear him ... somewhere above. The surface of the water was close above. There he moved cautiously in the shallows, he was diving, swimming to save her where she was trapped in the dark so she must guide him *I'm here I'm here I'M HERE*.

As the black water rose about her, to fill her lungs.

As the black water rose about her imperceptibly it seemed to her that draining, trickling water in thin rivulets like tears on her face, the soft groping-sucking of hundreds of leeches fastening their mouths on her, no it was merely water, she was sitting in water, shivering convulsively in water that smelled of sewage, gasoline, oil, her own urine where she'd soiled herself. *Don't leave me. I'm here.*

One minute speeding along the bouncy rutted road the moon bright overhead and his kiss hard on her mouth the next minute fighting for their lives and he'd kicked her convulsive himself in terror to escape but he had not known what he was doing, it was blind panic, she understood.

She understood. She had faith.

She remembered now who he was: The Senator.

She felt his fingertips on her bare shoulder, his breath that smelled of beer, alcohol ... she was not a bad girl, she would explain behaving, in The Senator's company, in such a way as to appear to be, or in fact to be, obvious, expected, banal.

Yet, after they'd been introduced, after they were talking so easily, discovering so much to

talk about, Carl Spader for instance, *Citizens'*
Inquiry for instance, Kelly had changed her
mind about the man.

—*really warm, gracious. Genuinely inter-*
ested in other people. And certainly intelligent.

Rehearsing the future, in words. Your words.
Your story.

For you must never doubt there will be a
future.

And such a sense of humor!

Making *him* laugh, entertaining him ... an
exhausted middle-aged man beginning to go soft
in the gut, steely-gray curly hair thinning at the
crown of his head, his left knee he'd sprained
back in January playing squash so, damn it, he's
easy game for Ray Annick on the court, wild
Ray with his lethal second serve, yes make me
laugh entertain me I want so badly to be happy
so Kelly Kelleher was inspired telling the story
(which she'd told Buffy long ago but sweet
Buffy pretended to be hearing it for the first
time) of the Gowanda Heights feud, no it was
more than a feud it was outright war, property
holders in the township were forced to choose
sides and no waffling was permitted: either you
favored the Gowanda Heights "tradition" of unpaved roads (which were surprisingly costly—a
minimum of $40,000 a year on the average per
road above the cost of maintaining paved roads)
or you favored "modernization" and there were

stormy emotions on both sides of the issue but especially on the side of the traditionalists ... like Artie Kelleher of Scotch Pine Way, who believed his property values would decline if his road was paved and who quarreled so bitterly with an old friend who opposed him at the township hearings that Kelly's mother feared he might have a heart attack. Friendships were shattered, neighbors stopped speaking, lawsuits were threatened, at least one dog was suspected of being poisoned ... and all for what, Kelly demanded laughing, all for *what*: dirt roads!

The Senator laughed but well, yes, he supposed he understood, you have to know the human heart, the cherished trivia of the human heart, there *is* nothing not political as Thomas Mann said no matter how petty how selfish how ignorant it seems to neutral observers, Kelly was too young to understand, maybe.

"Young? I'm not young at all. I don't feel young at all."

The words sudden and fierce, and her laughter rather fierce, so that the others looked at her; *he* looked at her.

She was determined not to say *Senator I wrote my senior honors thesis on you* unless the statement could be supremely casual, amusing.

23

SHE WAS PULLING HERSELF UP USING THE STEERING wheel as a lever.

She was trembling with the effort, whimpering like a small sick frightened child.

Like a child pleading *Help me. Don't forget me. I'm here.*

How many minutes had passed since the car ran off the road, was it fifteen minutes?—forty minutes?—she could not gauge for some of this time she had not been fully conscious waking suddenly in terror as something snakelike rushed across her face, her neck, soaking her hair, not a snake and not anything truly alive but a gushing coil of black water as the car which had been apparently precariously balanced on its side shifted with the pressure of the current to overturn completely.

Now trapped in here, not knowing where *here* was, not knowing how far away *he* was, upside down in utter blackness squirming and panting trying to get free groping for—what?—the steering wheel—her stiff fingers grasping the broken wheel to use as a lever as *he* had used it as a lever working himself free.

The steering wheel positioned her at least. She could not see but she could calculate: how far to the driver's door that would open for her, she was certain it would, it must, open for *her* as it had opened for *him*, not wanting to think that perhaps the door had been flung open partly by the collision with the guardrail and had subsequently been shut by the force of the current, the rapid churning water she could not see but feel, hear, smell, sense with every pore of her being: her enemy, it was: a predator, it was: her Death.

Not wanting to think. To acknowledge.

You're not an optimist, you're dead.

She was telling her mother she was a good girl but her mother seemed not to hear, speaking quickly, as if embarrassed, her grave gray eyes Kelly had always thought so lovely fixed on a spot behind Kelly's shoulder, "that sort of love is just a"—Kelly could not hear but thought it might be *a fever in the blood*—"it doesn't last, it can't last. Darling, I don't even remember when your father and I ... the last time ... like that ... that ..."—now profoundly embarrassed but pressing bravely onward for this was the conversation they had had, Kelly remembered suddenly, when, aged sixteen, at that time in her third year at the Bronxville Academy, she had fallen desperately in love with a boy and they had made love awkwardly and miserably Kelly for the first time and subsequently the boy avoided her and Kelly had wanted to die, could not sleep could not eat could not endure she was certain, like one of her friends at the school who had made in fact a serious suicide attempt swallowing a full container of barbiturates washed down with a pint of whiskey and taken by ambulance to the emergency room of Bronxville General she'd had her stomach pumped out, her frail life saved, and Kelly Kelleher did not want to die really, crying in Mother's arms she swore she did not want to die she was a good girl really, she was not a bad girl really, she did not want to take the birth-control pill like the other girls, and Mother was comforting her, Mother was there to comfort her, even now though not seeming to hear her (because of the rushing of the water perhaps, the barrier of the wind-shield) yes Mother was there to comfort her.

As the black water splashed over her mouth.

Except by a sudden exertion of strength she would not have known she'd had after the initial dazed trauma she was able to lift herself partway free of whatever it was clamping her knee, and now there was her foot, her right foot entirely without sensation, as it was invisible to her as if it did not exist and perhaps it was severed . . . except if so she would have bled to death by now she reasoned, so much time had passed.

Still, she could neither move the toes of that foot nor feel them and even the physiological concepts of *toes*, *foot* had become confused in her mind so quickly she stopped thinking about them: she was an optimist.

Kelly imagines she's so cynical, so wise to the ways of the world her friends teased her fondly, *Oh but we know better!* unable to resist teasing her about the Dukakis debacle, and her stubborn loyalty to Carl Spader, who treated her like a typist, once at a party she'd overheard Jane Freiberg telling a man *Yes that's Kelly Kelleher let me introduce you she's so really sweet once you get past the*—and she'd turned away quickly not wanting to hear the rest of Jane's words.

So rude, people talking of her while she was within earshot. While she was alive.

Her friends speaking of her so. How did they dare!

Kelly?—beautiful.

A voice jarringly close in her ear. But she saw no face.

Nor could she remember his name exactly except to know that he was laboring to get to her, swimming against the swift choppy current his hair lifting in tendrils from his pale anguished face, he was reaching for the door handle, his fingers groping for the door handle that would release her if she had faith if she did not give in to fear to panic to terror to Death.

Here. I'm here.

Somehow it had happened she was lying upside down across what she understood to be the ceiling of the wrecked car, the roof was now resting rocking as if shuddering against the invisible creekbed, and close above her cramping her was the cushioned seat to which in some way she was still attached too, a strap across her shoulder, across her neck *failure of the spinal cord to fracture as the prisoner falls so that the prisoner slowly suffocates* but it was her right leg that was caught fast in the twisted metal: her foot paralyzed, numb, as empty of sensation as if it were a rock: severed? or still attached?

But no, she must not think of that. She was an optimist.

She realized then that she had vomited on herself without knowing when, reasoning swiftly that such a purging was beneficent clearing her stomach so that there would be less poison to pump out of it, this water that was not water of the sort with which she was familiar, transparent, faintly blue, clear and delicious not that sort of water but an evil muck-water, thick, viscous, tasting of sewage, gasoline, oil.

Here? Help me—.

Holding herself up out of the seeping water by sheer tremulous force gripping the steering wheel, whimpering like a child with the effort understanding *If I can keep my head up, my mouth clear* she would be able to suck at the air bubble floating above her irradiated by moonlight.

That bright flat moon! Proof, so long as she could see it, that she was still alive.

We'll get there Kelly. And we'll get there on time.

She knew, she understood, they were counting on her. *He* was counting on her.

There would be an ambulance. A siren. The red light spinning wildly bouncing careening through the marshland.

The girl named Lisa, the girl with a twin sister, who had tried to kill herself swallowing thirty-eight barbiturate tablets. They'd come to get her and pumped her stomach out and saved her and all the girls whispered in awe of her afterward her absence in classes and in the dining hall so conspicuous.

That girl, though a twin, a sister, was *not* Kelly Kelleher.

Kelly Kelleher who, after G——, vowed she would never take her life for all life is precious.

And so it was a matter of her strength, her will. The concentration of her soul. Not to give in. Not to weaken. The black water was rising by choppy degrees to splash over her chin, her mouth, but *If I can keep my head up* it was a matter of knowing what to do and doing it.

Why had she hesitated to say they were lost, why hadn't she told him to turn the car around, to reverse their course, oh please!—but she had not dared offend him.

The black water was her fault, she knew. You just don't want to offend them. Even the nice ones.

He *was* nice. Even knowing they were so closely watching, memorizing him, certain of his remarks, his jokes. The way, in the spontaneous heat of a tennis volley, he gripped his jaws tight, bared his teeth.

You come to despise your own words in your ears ... your "celebrity."

And how unexpectedly sweet he'd been to her. Kelly Kelleher. So radiant and assured there on the beach, wearing her new glamorously dark sunglasses the lenses scientifically treated to eliminate ultraviolet rays, and she knew she looked good, she was not a beautiful girl but sometimes you know, it's your time and you know, no happiness quite like that happiness.

You're an American girl: you know.

Yes she'd gained back a good deal of the weight. No her hair was no longer coming out in distressing handfuls, it was gleaming again, glossy, her mother would be relieved. A bitter childish thing to have wished G—— dead but *Of course I don't feel that way any longer, I think of you as a friend.*

Still she had hesitated not wanting to utter aloud the word *lost*, had her own mother not warned her no man will tolerate being made a fool of by any woman no matter how truthfully she speaks no matter how he loves her.

And then suddenly it was all right: the air bubble had stabilized.

So strangely shaped, luminous it seemed to her, her blinded eyes, bobbing against the seats now suspended from the ceiling but *it has stopped leaking away* she was certain, she would hold it fast to her sucking lips sucking like an infant's lips until help came to save her.

24

ALMOST STERNLY, REPROACHFULLY HE WAS SAYING, "—the Gulf War has given your generation a tragic idea of war and of diplomacy: the delusion that war is relatively easy, and diplomacy *is* war, the most expedient of options."

And though she was flattered, how could she fail to be flattered by a famous man addressing her so earnestly, and paying so little attention to the others, quickly she said, "There is no such thing as 'my' generation, Senator. We're divided by race, class, education, politics—even sexual self-definition. The only thing that links us is our—separateness."

The Senator considered this remark, thoughtfully.

The Senator nodded, thoughtfully. And smiled. "Well, then! I stand corrected, eh?"

Smiling at her. Frankly staring. What was the girl's name?—it was clear to all that indeed The Senator was impressed with the attractive articulate friend of the girl with whom Ray Annick was currently sleeping.

And how raw and beautiful this northern shore of Grayling Island—the smell of the salt air, the bright fresh open ocean, the saw-toothed and precipitous white-capped waves so beautiful this world you want to sink your teeth into it, thrust yourself up to the hilt in it, oh Christ.

25

KELLY, KELLY!—SHE HEARD HER NAME BEING CALLED from above, *Kelly!* now on all sides of her, loud, jarring, her name rippling through the black water.

Here, I'm here. Here.

As the water splashed and churned about her mouth, foul-tasting water not water, like no water she knew. But she was holding her head as high as she could, her neck trembling with the effort. She had pushed her face, her mouth, into a pocket of waning air in a space she could not have named except vaguely to indicate that it was beyond the passenger's seat of the capsized vehicle, beneath the glove compartment?—a space where her knees had been when she'd been sitting. Her knees, her feet.

Except she could no longer think of what the space was really. She had not the words, nor the logic by which they were joined.

Nor had she the word for *air* just knowing, sensing, that her sucking pursed lips must not lose it.

As the moonlit patch of light swelled, and ebbed, and swelled, and ebbed, she had no name for what was *light*, not even *life*.

As the black water filled her lungs, and she died.

No: she was watching the men playing tennis. She, Felicia Ch'en, Stacey Miles, amid the prickly wild rose above the St. Johns' handsome court, Kelly fingering the rose petals, stroking the thorns, sinking her nails into the fleshy red berries, a nervous mannerism, one of her bad habits, hard to break because it was barely conscious, watching the energetic play, watching him. Stacey said, laughing, "The main difference is, I mean you can see it so clearly, their *muscles*. Look at their *legs*."

The Senator was the tallest man on the court since Lucius from M.I.T. disguised his height playing out of a deep canny crouch, the young women admired, applauded, took snapshots, drifted away and returned and it *was* fascinating how a man will reveal his truest self, or so it seems, on the tennis court competing with other men, serious doubles is the real test, a risky enterprise. The Senator and his lawyer-friend Ray Annick gamely and good-naturedly teamed up, their opponents young enough to be their sons, *as a man ages the legs go first* but the shrewd player knows to conserve his limited energy and to force others to expend theirs, The Senator moved with territorial ease on the court, the manner of one who has played tennis since boyhood, years of instruction thus wicked shots to the rear of his opponents' court, amazing shots that barely skimmed the net, serves executed with machinelike precision placed seemingly where willed, and, yes, Kelly and the other spectators were impressed, they were admiring, noting how gentlemanly The Senator was calling certain of his opponents' balls *in* when they looked clearly *out*.

Good sportsmanship. In some, it's as hard to win gracefully as it is to lose.

But as game followed game the balance of authority gradually shifted, Lucius with his bizarre first serves and Stacey's lover with his dogged rushes to the net and unpredictable backhand wore The Senator and Ray Annick down, the sun too and the gusty wind and the St. Johns' court that needed repair, Kelly slipped tactfully away before the final set ended not wanting The Senator to see her observing, as, smiling in defeat, making a joke of it, he shook his young opponents' hands, not wanting to hear what the men said to one another, at such times, as a way of not saying other things.

No: she was walking along the beach her hair whipping in the wind, the yellow mesh tunic loose over the white swimsuit and her long legs smooth, strong, pinkened by the sun. She was walking along the beach and beside her was the tall broad-shouldered handsome man, big bear-like man, gray-grizzled curly hair, a famous face yet a comfortable face, a sunflower face, a kindly face, an uncle's face—the blue eyes so blue so keenly so intensely blue a blue like washed glass.

How keen, how intense his interest in Kelly Kelleher. How flattering.

Asking her about her work with Carl Spader, her background, her life; nodding emphatically saying yes he'd read her article on capital punishment in *Citizens' Inquiry*—he was certain he'd read it.

Curious too, though he kept his tone casual, with a crinkled avuncular smile, if she had a boyfriend at the present time?

And if she'd ever been attracted to working in Washington?

And if she might consider joining his staff—sometime?

Murmured Kelly Kelleher, flushed with pleasure, yet level-headed too like any lawyer's daughter, "That depends, Senator."

Of course.

How canny The Senator had been at the 1988 Democratic convention, declining Michael Dukakis's offer of the vice-presidential candidacy. Let Bentsen have the second-best position, paired with the absurd Quayle, *he* would have the presidential nomination, or nothing. Yet more canny, not at that time to have very actively pursued the nomination himself since he'd understood, as Dukakis had not, that the Democrats' best efforts in that election year were doomed.

As Kelly Kelleher had not understood. Those Reagan years, the dismal spiritual debasement, the hypocrisy, cruelty, lies uttered with a cosmetic smile ... surely, the American people would *see*.

Yet it had been Kelly who'd been blind, and what a fool. Laughing about it now on this Fourth of July years later strolling with a United States senator passing miniature American flags set in the sand by the children of Buffy's neighbors, making of her exhaustion and heartbreak an amusing anecdote to tell against herself.

But The Senator did not laugh. He said, vehemently, "Oh Christ. I know. *I* wanted to die, nearly, when Stevenson lost to Eisenhower—I loved that man."

Kelly Kelleher was startled to hear such an admission. A man loving another man?

Even in political terms?

The Senator spoke of Adlai Stevenson and Kelly listened attentively. She had an imprecise, however respectful, knowledge of Stevenson, for of course she had studied that era in American history, the Eisenhower years, the Eisenhower phenomenon her professor had called it, but she did not want to be tested. She did not want to allude to her father's contempt for the man and she could not even recall whether there had been a single campaign, or two. In the early 1950s?

Cautiously she inquired, "Did you work for him, Senator?"

"The second time, yes. In nineteen fifty-six. I was a sophomore at Harvard. The first time— when he might actually have won—I was just a kid."

"And were you always—political?"

He bared his big teeth in a happy smile, for clearly this was his question.

" 'The state is a creation of nature, and man is a political animal'—by nature."

He was quoting—was it Aristotle?

Kelly Kelleher who had been drinking an

unaccustomed amount of beer much of the afternoon laughed happily too. As if this were a fact to be celebrated. It was the wind whipping her hair, it was the beauty of the island. Grayling Island. Maine. The pounding surf like a narcotic, the high-banked beach, pebbly sand stretching for miles festooned with wild rose and the enormous wind-sculpted dunes, those curious creases or ripples in them as if a giant rake had been combed through them with infinite care. How blessed was Kelly Kelleher's life, to have brought her *here*!

It was unlike her to be so bold, so flirtatious. Asking The Senator archly, " 'Man'—and not woman? Isn't 'woman' a political animal too?"

"Some women. Sometimes. We know that. But, most of the time, women find politics boring. The power-play of male egos. Like war. Eh? Boring in its monotony, beneath all the turmoil?"

But Kelly was not to be led. As if this were a seminar, and Kelly Kelleher one of the stars, she said, frowning, "Women can't afford to think of politics as 'boring'! Not at this point in history. The Supreme Court, abortion—"

They were walking much slower now. They were breathless, excited.

The tender soles of Kelly's feet stung from the heat of the white-glaring sand. Yet the wind was raising tiny goose bumps on her arms: it must have been twenty-five degrees cooler here than back in Boston.

The Senator, noticing the goose bumps, drew a forefinger gently along her arm. Kelly shivered the more at his touch.

"Are you cold, dear?—that thing you're wearing is so flimsy."

"No. No, I'm fine."

"Would you like to turn back?"

"Of course not."

Touching her arm. That sudden intimacy. Standing so close, staring down at her.

Deliberately, slowly as if with exaggerated courtesy The Senator gripped Kelly Kelleher's shoulders, stooped to kiss her, and her eyelids fluttered, she was genuinely startled, surprised, yes and excited too, for how swiftly this was happening, how swiftly after all, yet as he kissed her after the first moment she stood her ground firmly, heels dug into the crusty sand, she leaned to the man taking the kiss as if it were her due, a natural and inevitable and desired development of their conversation. And bold too, giddy too, parrying his tongue with her teeth.

How nice. How nice, really. You can't deny—how nice.

As the black water filled her lungs, and she died.

26

EXCEPT: AMID BLINDING LIGHTS SUDDENLY SHE WAS being wheeled on a gurney flat on her back strapped in place amid lights and strangers' eyes and that harsh hospital smell they were pumping the black water out of her lungs, the poisonous muck out of her stomach, her very veins, in a matter of minutes! seconds! the team of them, an emergency room crew, strangers to the dying girl yet she was of such enormous concern to them you would have thought it was one of their own being resuscitated, and how swiftly! how without hesitation! she was trying to explain to them that she was awake, she was conscious, please don't hurt me, how terrifying the clamps that held her fast on the table and her head gripped firmly by the gloved hands of someone who stood behind her and the hose forced down her throat, the thick fat hideous hose that was so long, so long, you would not believe how long and how much pain scraping the back of her mouth, her throat, choking her so she wanted to vomit but could not vomit, she wanted to scream but could not scream and in the midst of a convulsion her heart lurched and stopped and she died, she was dying but they were ready, of course they were ready, elated by this challenge they were ready scarcely missing a beat of her faltering heart they stimulated it with powerful electric jolts. Ah! yes! good! again! like that! again! yes! and the dying girl was revived, the young female corpse was revived, the heart's pumping restored within five seconds and oxygen restored to the brain, and by degrees the marmoreal skin took on the flush of color, of life: the eyes leaked tears: and out of Death there came this life: hers.

Don't let Lisa die, dear God don't let her die, don't don't she was waiting in the outer room, she and several others, *Oh God please* in that calm of mutual hysteria three or four of them, girls from the residence hall, and the dorm resident who was only a few years older, Kelly Kelleher was the one who'd seen Lisa Gardiner collapse in the bathroom, Kelly Kelleher was the one who'd run screaming to the resident's suite, now keeping vigil in the waiting room beyond the emergency room of Bronxville General and the shock of it, the trauma of it, seeing one of their own carried out on a stretcher unconscious and open-eyed open-mouthed her tongue convulsing drooling as in an epileptic fit and Kelly Kelleher staring, knuckles pressed to her mouth, had thought, *Why it isn't Lisa's life it's simply—life* seeing how it was draining away in her like water down a sink and perhaps she was already dead and could they restore that life to her?

Could, and did.

Later, they'd learned, and some of them resented it, that Lisa Gardiner and her twin sister Laura (whom they had never met—Laura went to school at the Concord Academy in Massachusetts) had tried to kill themselves by taking sleeping pills in a suicide pact, three years before when they were living at home, and in eighth grade in a public junior high school in Snyder, New York.

Why did some of the girls resent this fact?—because the near-death of Lisa had disturbed them so, churned them up so, there was no subject except Lisa and the emergency team rushing up the stairs and into the bathroom and carrying Lisa away and the fact that strictly speaking Lisa had died, her heart had stopped, and how weird! how terrible! how amazing! and you grew simply to resent it, all that fuss over Lisa Gardiner who always had to be the center of attention, and all that fuss over death, and dying, how exhausting by the end of the term!

When Lisa returned for a visit, Kelly Kelleher was the one who made a point to be friendly with her, yes and to talk earnestly with her, the two girls who had not been particularly close or confiding previously now observed in an intense conversation in the lounge and what was Lisa Gardiner saying, why was Kelly Kelleher so fascinated, Lisa with her rather low forehead, her nose too wide at its tip as if she were continually sniffing in finicky disdain, Kelly with her peaked, pretty face, her somber mouth—"There isn't that much difference between people, and there isn't that much *purpose* to people," Lisa was saying in a flat, nasal, bemused, bullying voice, "—if you're one-half of a twin set you *know*."

No I don't, no I reject that I reject you, I am not your sister, I am not your twin, I am not you.

27

SHE COULD HEAR THE SIREN. SHE COULD SEE THE AM-
bulance speeding along the sandy rutted nameless road, the red light on its roof spinning like
a top.

She was gagging, the hose already in her
mouth. A snaky black hose so thick! so long! you
wouldn't believe how long! Lisa had giggled.

Stretching her arms, out, out ... That look
of radiant madness in her eyes and *she was licking her lips*.

Wild! Buffy St. John had said, years later.
That's really sick.

Buffy had pinched her, Buffy's teasing-pinch

that, damn it, *hurt*. Saying, pouting, as Kelly Kelleher was hastily stuffing her things into her suitcase, Yes but why leave *now*, can't you leave a little later?—and Kelly Kelleher murmured, Oh Buffy—I'm sorry, that sunburnt flush on her throat, face, knowing how Buffy would speak of her afterward, not of The Senator but of her, Kelly Kelleher I thought was my friend, for Christ's sake—! But Kelly was too embarrassed to say what both she and Buffy knew.

If I don't do as he asks there won't be any later.

As he kissed her those several times, kissing, sucking, groping as if, though they were standing fully clothed on a beach that, though not very populated, was nonetheless not deserted, he was in an agony to find a way into her, she felt the jolt of desire: not her desire, but the man's. As, since girlhood, kissing and being kissed, Kelly Kelleher had always felt, not her own, but the other's, the male's, desire. Quick and galvanizing as an electric shock.

Feeling too, once she caught her breath, that familiar wave of anxiety, guilt—*I've made you want me, now I can't refuse you.*

Close up, Kelly saw that The Senator was not a handsome nor even perhaps a healthy man exactly: his skin was very flushed, unevenly mot-

tled, tiny broken capillaries in the nose and
cheeks, and his eyes, that distinctive blue but
the lids were somewhat puffy, the large staring
eyeballs threaded with blood. He was sweating,
almost panting as if he'd been running and was
out of condition.

"Kelly. Beautiful Kelly."

And when Kelly could think of no reply,
adding: "What am I going to do with you,
Kelly?—so early in the day, am I going to lose
you?"

One of his aides had gotten him a room in a
motel in Boothbay Harbor, not an easy accom-
plishment on the Fourth of July, but he had the
room, he'd checked in, it was waiting for him
and where was Kelly Kelleher staying the night?

At Buffy's of course. Kelly was a house
guest of Buffy's planning to stay the full weekend: until Sunday.

The Senator's manner was bemused, not at
all coercive. Just bemused. Asking her another
time, as if he'd forgotten he had already asked,
if she had a boyfriend? a fiancé? one of the men
at the party? that interesting young black from
M.I.T. perhaps?

The Senator's navy blue knit sports shirt fit-
ted his upper arms tightly and was damp with
perspiration. His seersucker trousers were rum-
pled at the rear.

An odor about him of beer, after-shave cologne, frank male sweat. Kelly's nostrils pinched half-pleasurably. She smiled.

Explaining now sobbing and angry to both her parents that she was not a bad girl, truly she was not. The man was married but not living with his wife and it was the wife who wanted the separation, the wife who had *asked me to leave, kicked me out,* fortunately both their children were adults now and capable of assessing the situation for themselves, a man like The Senator with a love of life a love of people both men and women a zest for meeting new people for exchanging views an appetite for ... perhaps it was appetite itself.

Biting, sucking the very marrow. Thrusting yourself into it to the hilt. *Christ how otherwise do you know you're alive?*

Mr. Kelleher understood, it seemed. Yes Daddy you'd be a goddamned hypocrite not to.

Mrs. Kelleher was upset, distraught. Kelly squirmed with guilt seeing that look in her mother's face but it made her fucking angry too. Mommy just stop thinking about me, that way I mean. My girlfriends' mothers—they handle it perfectly well.

The difference is, Kelly, I love you.

Oh hell. Give me a break.

I love you, I don't want you ever ever to

be hurt Kelly that's the one thing I want to shield you from, that was my thought ... you might not believe this but that was my actual thought ... when they gave me to you, in the hospital when you were born, and I knew you were a girl and I was never so happy in all my life before or since, I vowed I would never let my daughter be hurt as I have been hurt I will give my life for her I swear to You God.

Mommy was crying, and Kelly was crying, turning her head from side to side spitting and gagging, tasting the oil, the gasoline, the sewage, not entirely certain any longer where she was, why her spine so twisted, both her legs twisted, she was upside down was she?—in the dark not knowing where is up, the pressure of the black water on all sides now, churning, rising, eager to fill her mouth, and her lungs.

Saying, relenting, *All right Mommy I guess so. Yes.*

Take me home from here Mommy. I'm here.

It was not clear whether Mr. and Mrs. Kelleher had been summoned to the scene of the accident and were standing now on the embankment as the car was being lifted out of the creek; or whether they were already at the hospital, waiting outside the emergency room. Kelly was puzzled too seeing their faces not as she remembered them, but so young—so attractive. Her own age?

Mommy such a beauty, her face unlined, her eyes so clear—and that stiff-glazed bouffant hair, so silly so regal!

Daddy so handsome, and so lanky!—and his hair, my God his hair, thick and curly and coppery-brown like Kelly's own, as she had not seen it in years.

Yes she'd loved them all her life even more now in her own precarious adulthood than previously but how do you say such a fact?—how choose the words?—and when of all occasions should they be uttered?

Mommy, Daddy hey I love you, you know that I hope, please don't let me die I love you, okay?

She was running in her little white anklet socks on Grandma's prickly carpet having kicked off her shiny new patent-leather shoes, squealing giggling as the quick hard hands swooped from behind to lift her, it's always a surprise how hard, how strong another's hands are, a man's hands, and he cried *Who's this! who's this! mmmm who's this little angel-bee who's this!* lifting the kicking squealing child high above his head so his arms trembled and afterward she overheard Mommy and Grandma scolding him about his blood pressure, what on earth are you doing you might have dropped her.

He'd winked at her. Grandpa loved her so.

And now she tasted cold, and the unspeakable horror of her situation washed over her: if the black water filled her lungs, and she died, and the news came to her parents and grandparents, they would die, too.

Oh God no, oh no. That can't be.

They loved Kelly so, they would die, too.

Except realizing then suddenly, a bit of relief: Grandpa Ross *was* dead, himself—so he'd be spared, knowing.

And maybe they would not need to tell Grandma?—Kelly saw no need, frankly she saw no need.

Mommy you see my point don't you?— okay?

Daddy?

Okay?

28

EVERYWHERE ON GRAYLING ISLAND THERE GREW, RUN-
ning low against the earth, wild rose, flowering
wild rose, beautiful rosy-lavender petals and
spiny treacherous stems, sharp thorns Kelly
drew her fingertips absentmindedly against watching the men play tennis ... *Rosa rugosa* it was,
or was it *Rosa virginiana*.

Wild rose, everywhere. Blooming. Festooning
the dun-colored beach.

And the fruit of the bushes, like tiny plums,
beautiful too, a blood-swollen look to them, an
erotic look, these too Kelly touched, running
her fingertips over them, digging in her nails.

Rosehips, The Senator said. Taking pleasure in speaking of them, his grandmother steeping them to make rosehip tea, did Kelly like rosehip tea? herbal teas were very popular today, eh? and his grandmother had made jam, too, from the rosehips, he thought. Unless he was confusing it with something else.

Rosehips, or maybe currants. Huckleberries.

In the kitchen Buffy grimaced emptying ice cubes into a container saying, "You and The Senator are getting along very well," with a sidelong smile, and Kelly Kelleher smiled too, feeling her face heat, murmuring, "Well," and there was a pause, and another barrage of ice cubes crashing into the plastic container, then Buffy said something so very Buffylike, you never knew from which direction Buffy was coming, was it a sly sort of joke, a nudging complicity, was it a warning, was it that prickly sort of insult you didn't quite absorb until later, or, simply, bluntly, a statement of fact, "Don't forget, he voted to give aid to the Contras."

29

KELLY? KELLY? COME TO ME.

She could hear him, suddenly. Shouting, somewhere close overhead, tugging at the door on the driver's side of the car, making the car rock with his strength.

She tried to speak but water filled her mouth, she shook her head, spat the water out, *I'm here, I'm here, help me,* pulling herself up by sheer tremulous strength of her left arm, the small compact muscle of her left arm, the shoulder, she was trembling with the effort, how many minutes? or had it been hours? time did not pass in this place submerged in black water

except as it was recorded in the water's gradual
rising, the cruel methodical rising, a digital
watch's clicking, and would The Senator see her
here?—in such blackness?—in this trap, this pit,
this coffin, whatever it was, the name for it lost,
squeezing her so small, so tight, so cramped you
had to be crippled, your spine bent back upon
itself to fit into it?

Her head, now she was awake, was livid
with pain. Splotches of light like tumorous
growths behind her eyes, tight-impacted in her
skull. It seemed that her face had lost all sensation, she'd held her lips so pursed for so long,
gasping, sucking, the air bubble floated away
teasing and cruel as a living capricious thing,
bobbing and drifting this way, and now that
way, and again this way, so she strained, sobbing
with the effort, to reach it.

I'm here. I'm here. Here!

He had dived into the black water to rescue her
but he was far away, and everything was so dark,
blind. And she understood she'd offended him,
and the insult was irrevocable.

Her lips playfully shut against his tongue.
The ease of it she'd imagined, the banter, the
mutual regard, respect, he *did* respect her she
knew, she knew, and then reluctantly parting
her lips, his fat thrusting tongue, the hunger in
him.

The shame of it, how desperate she'd been clutching at the man's trouser leg, at his shoe! As he'd kicked to get free! His shoe, soaked, in her hand.

His shoe!

Oh Kelly, her girlfriends would laugh, Buffy would shriek with laughter wiping her eyes, —his *shoe*!

Limping one shoe on one shoe off fleeing on foot back along the marshland road to the highway from which they'd turned off where there was sure to be a 7-Eleven store, a gas station, a tavern with an outdoor telephone booth.

No. It had not happened yet. The sun blazing late in the afternoon, this long hilarious day like a pinwheel inexhaustibly throwing off sparks.

The splendid American flag all flapping silk red-white-and-blue at the top of Edgar St. John's flagpole. The tallest flagpole on Derry Road, very possibly on Grayling Island.

My daddy's a patriot, Buffy said. Served in the C.I.A. for twenty years and didn't get his ass blown off.

It had not happened yet because there again was Buffy arranging her guests so she could take Polaroid pictures. Buffy in jeans and bikini top her "faux" ponytail sleek and blackly gleaming falling to the middle of her back, her lewd green-taloned nails curved about the camera, tongue protruding between glistening white teeth. Oh please be still will you, look up here please—and you, Senator, mmm?—like that! Great!

There were several Polaroids of The Senator standing at a picnic table, one foot on the bench, an elbow on his seersucker knee and a casual pose it was, Kelly Kelleher close by as if in the crook of his arm, laughing into the camera's eye as the flash popped, and The Senator was smiling guardedly, a tucked-in sort of smile, an almost-meditative smile, a smile of the kind that retracts even as it expands, something in the eyes deflected too, grave, as if the man were pondering what caption might be inserted beneath this festive Fourth of July pose to be transmitted by wire service through the United States and numerous foreign countries, featured on network television news?

But no, you can't imagine your future. Even that it is yours.

One shoe on, one shoe off. Limping. Drenched and shivering and murmuring aloud Oh God. Oh God. Oh God.

30

. . . FIVE MEANS OF CAPITAL PUNISHMENT REMAINING in the United States at the present time. Recent Supreme Court rulings, states' rights. Overwhelming support of death penalty in polls. *Why?—because it's a deterrent. Because it sends out the message: Life isn't cheap.* Five means of which the oldest is hanging. Last used in Kansas, 1965. Condemned man took sixteen minutes to die, sometimes it's longer. Still an option in Montana. *The only kind of deterrent these animals understand.* Firing squad, Utah. Electric chair, introduced 1890, New York State. "Humane" alternative to hanging, firing squad:

condemned man (or woman) is strapped into chair, copper electrodes affixed to leg, shaved head. Executioner administers an initial jolt of between 500 and 2,000 volts for thirty seconds. *We're talking about hardened criminals here— murderers. The mentally and morally unfit.* If death fails to occur with the initial jolt, additional jolts are administered. Two, three, four. Some hearts are stronger than others. Accidents occur. Smoke, sometimes bluish-orange flames rise from the burning body. A smell as of cooking meat. As with hanging, eyeballs sometimes pop out of sockets to hang on cheeks. Vomiting, urination, defecation. Skin turns bright red blistering and swelling to the point of bursting like an overcooked frankfurter. Often, current is not strong enough and death is not "instantaneous" but by degrees. Prisoner is tortured to death. *Not decent civilized people like the kind we know but people who are a genuine threat to society, who must be stopped. If not, they will be given light prison sentences, paroled—to strike again!*

Gas chamber, introduced 1924, Nevada. A popular choice as a "humane" alternative. Condemned man (or woman) is strapped in chair, beneath the chair a bowl filled with sulfuric acid and distilled water into which sodium cyanide is dropped releasing hydrogen cyanide gas. Oxygen cut off from brain at once. Prisoner experiences extreme horror—strangulation. *The issue of race isn't the issue believe me, that's a smokescreen, maybe it's so that more black men have always been executed in the United States than white men, maybe it's a statistical fact that whites who kill blacks are less likely to receive the death penalty than blacks who kill whites, yes there's a big difference between states, counties, urban areas, rural areas, the prosecutor makes the charges maybe some of them are racists but you can't expect the criminal justice system to rectify the problems of society for God's sake.* Violent spasms as in an epileptic fit. Popping eyes. Skin turns purple. Not immediate toxic action on vital organs but asphyxiation is the cause of death. "Arguably the most barbaric and painful way to die." (Physician)

Death by lethal injection, newest and most enthusiastically promoted "humane" method of state-inflicted death. Invented 1977, pioneered in Oklahoma. Condemned man (or woman) is strapped to a hospital gurney, given a catheter needle dripping intravenous fluid into a vein. The first drug injected is sodium thiopental, a barbiturate; then 100 milligrams pavulon, muscle relaxant; potassium chloride to speed the process of death. *Some of these scientific ways these "merciful" ways are too good for those animals, I'm speaking of filthy beasts not of human beings. Why keep them alive, why feed them, cater to them, why shouldn't they suffer seeing the suffering they cause in others, why not "an eye for an eye a tooth for a tooth," tell me why? why not?* And lethal injection is low-cost, appeals to budget-conscious legislatures, favorite of capital punishment advocates since death is perceived as painless just falling asleep, society is absolved of charges of barbarism, the wish to torture, seek vengeance.

Quest for "humane" alternatives in death a quest not for the sake of the condemned but for the sake of American citizens that, in premeditated murder inflicted arbitrarily by the state, they be absolved of guilt ...

He'd flattered her, Elizabeth Anne Kelleher, saying, insisting, yes he was certain he'd read her article in *Citizens' Inquiry*—or, perhaps, one of his staff had given him a précis.

Why did you write on such a subject, The Senator asked, curious, and Kelly Kelleher paused not wanting to say that Carl Spader had suggested it to her, saying instead, It's a subject I've been interested in for a long time, the more research you do into it the more disgusted you feel. Which was true, too.

Her quarrels with her father notwithstanding.

"Eye for an eye, tooth for a tooth"—why not? Crude, maybe, primitive maybe, but it

sends the message that life isn't cheap—why not?

Certainly The Senator was on record opposed to the death penalty.

Certainly he was bravely at odds with many in his home state, where capital punishment, by electrocution, was still on the books; where there were still condemned prisoners on Death Row, exhausting their appeals, waiting to die.

Certainly he'd made speeches. He'd been eloquent. As politically adamant as his friend Mario Cuomo. Capital punishment is unacceptable in a civilized society because the taking of any life for any purpose is loathsome, reducing society to the primitive level of the murderer himself. And, most frightful of all, considering the wildly arbitrary nature of the American criminal justice system there is always the possibility of innocent men (and women) being sentenced to death ... from which punitive fate, unlike any other, there can be no return.

31

AM I READY?

Packing her things in haste as the evening before she'd unpacked them carefully, ceremoniously as if this room on Grayling Island with its strawberry floral wallpaper and chaste white organdy bed were a sacred place she forgot completely from one visit to the other, and now it was a place from which, by her own eager effort, she was being expelled.

The plan was to slip away from Buffy's at precisely 7 P.M. to catch the 7:30 P.M. ferry to Boothbay Harbor but a new carload of guests had just driven up and The Senator was having another drink intense in conversation so perhaps they would not make that ferry, and when was the next?—no matter, there is always a next.

Don't expect anything, really. Whatever it is, it is. And that will be enough.

Practical-minded Kelly Kelleher, sternly admonishing herself.

Still, her hands were trembling. Her breath was quickened. In that heart-shaped white-wicker-framed mirror over the bureau a girl's face floated rapt, glowing, hopeful.

In all truthfulness her mind did fly free like a maverick kite drunkenly climbing the air above the sand dunes thinking he *is* after all separated from his wife, his marriage *is* after all over—he says; voters are no longer puritanical, punitive.

To avoid the appearance of impropriety. The appearance of extramarital scandal.

It's a changed world from the one you knew, Mother. I wish you would accept that.

I wish you would let me alone!

Carrying a beer as she'd passed through the kitchen where Ray Annick was on the telephone speaking in a low, angry voice, the words *asshole, fuck, fucking* punctuating his customarily fastidious speech, Kelly was startled for here was a man so unlike the genial smiling man romantically attentive to Buffy St. John all that day,

so unlike the man courteous and sweetly attentive to Kelly Kelleher, and she saw that his eyes
(which were puffy, glazed—he'd been drinking
all afternoon and the tennis games had humbled
him) followed her as she passed a few yards
from him, as a cat's eyes follow movement with
an instinctive impersonal predatory interest; yet,
as soon as she passed beyond his immediate
field of vision he ceased to see her, ceased to
register her existence.

"Look, I fucking *told* you—we'll take this
up on Monday. For Christ's sake!"

Kelly Kelleher teetering on one leg, swiftly
changing out of her white spandex swimsuit.
Purchased at Lord & Taylor, midsummer sale,
the previous Saturday.

Swiftly changing into a summer knit shift,
pale lemony stripes, cut up high on the shoulders revealing her lovely smooth bare shoulders,
that shoulder, that tingling area of skin, he'd
touched with his tongue.

Had that really happened, Kelly Kelleher
wondered.

Would it happen again. Again.

You love your life because it's yours.

The wind in the tall broom-headed rushes,
those rushes that looked so like human figures.
Blond, swaying. At the periphery of vision.

The wind, the cold easterly wind off the

Atlantic. Shivering rippling water like pale flame
striking the beach, pounding the beach. Buffy
said that the highest dunes they were looking
at were seventy feet high, and how weird they
were, the dunes where the pitch pines can't
keep them from migrating, roaming loose over
the Island like actual waves of the ocean with
their own crests and troughs and it's been mea-
sured that they move west to east at the rate of
between ten and fifteen feet a year, over Derry
Road so it has to be cleaned off, right through
the snow fences and over the beach grass—"It's
beautiful here but, you know," shivering, wincing, "—it has nothing to do with human wishes."

And now it was short choppy waves she
was hearing against the slanted roof of this
room—snug and safe beneath the covers, Grandma's crocheted quilt with the pandas around the
border.

You love your life. You're ready.

She had not wanted to say yes. But she'd
wanted to say yes.

Yes to the ferry, to Boothbay Harbor. The
Boothbay Marriott, it was.

Beyond Boothbay, beyond the fifth of
July...?

Kelly Kelleher would make the man love
her. She knew how.

Surprising herself with this thought, and its
vehemence. *You're ready.*

In the car, she'd turned the radio dial, heard the reedy synthesized music all sound-tissue, no skeleton. How touching, The Senator a man of fifty-five felt such nostalgia for a youth so long ago!

Saying yes though she'd seen how The Senator had been drinking. At first he'd been prudent drinking white wine, Perrier water, low-calorie beer then he'd switched to the stronger stuff, he and Ray Annick: the two older men at the party.

Older men. Yes and they did think of themselves that way, you could tell.

It was the Fourth of July. A meaningless holiday now but one Americans all celebrate, or almost all Americans celebrate. Rockets' red glare, bombs bursting in air.

Which is how you know, isn't it—the flag is still there.

Turning onto the unpaved road, impatient, exuberant, the Toyota skidding in the sandy ruts but under control, The Senator was a practiced driver, quite enjoying the drive, the very impatience impelling it, the haste of their flight. Perhaps *lost* was their intention?

After a quick drink or two Kelly Kelleher had confessed to The Senator that she'd written her senior honors thesis on him at Brown, and instead of being annoyed, or embarrassed, or bored, The Senator had beamed with pleasure.

"You don't say! Why—I hope it was worth it!"

"Of course it was worth it, Senator."

They talked, they were talking animatedly, and others listened, Kelly Kelleher and The Senator, *taken with each other* as the phrase goes. Kelly heard herself tell The Senator what it was most about his ideas that excited her: his proposal to establish neighborhood liaison offices, especially in impoverished urban areas, so that citizens could communicate more directly with their elected officials; his proposals for day-care centers, free medical facilities, remedial education program; his support of the arts, community theater in particular. Passionately Kelly Kelleher spoke, and, with the mesmerized air of one staring, not at an individual, but at a vast audience, passionately The Senator listened. Had his words ever sounded quite so good to him, so reasonable and convincing?—so melodic, lyric, inspired? Kelly was reminded irreverently of a cynicism of Charles de Gaulle's frequently quoted by Carl Spader: *Since a politician never believes what he says, he is surprised when others believe him.*

Kelly broke off suddenly, self-consciously. "Senator, I'm sorry—you must have heard this sort of thing thousands of times."

And The Senator said, courteously, altogether seriously, "Yes, Kelly, perhaps—but never from *you.*"

In the near distance, at a neighbor's, the rackety noise of firecrackers. High overhead the flapping of the St. John family's shimmering American flag.

As the black water filled her lungs, and she died.

No: it was time for the feast: borne by the wind a delicious smell of grilling meat over which Ray Annick in a comical cook's hat and apron presided, swaying-drunk but funnily capable: slabs of marinated tuna, chicken pieces swabbed with Tex-Mex sauce, raw red patties of ground sirloin the size of pancakes. Corn on the cob, buckets of potato salad and coleslaw and bean salad and curried rice, quarts of Häagen-Dazs passed around with spoons. What appetite they had, especially the younger men! The Senator too ate ravenously, yet fastidiously, wiping his mouth with a paper napkin after nearly every bite.

Kelly, though so hungry she was light-headed, shaky, found it difficult to eat. She raised her fork to her mouth, then lowered it again. Though there were numerous others among Buffy's guests who would have liked to speak with The Senator, The Senator insisted upon focusing his attention upon Kelly Kelleher; as if, as in the most improbable of fairy tales, the man had made this impromptu trip to Grayling Island expressly to see *her*.

Heat stung pleasurably in Kelly Kelleher's cheeks. It crossed her mind that Carl Spader would be most impressed, yes and frankly jealous, to hear about this meeting.

The Senator winced as a string of firecrackers exploded next door.

Kelly thought, He fears being shot—assassination.

What a novelty, to be so public a figure one fears *being assassinated*!

The Senator said, "I really don't like the Fourth of July, I guess. Since I was a little boy I've associated it with the turning point of summer. Half through, and now moving toward fall." He spoke with a curious bemused melancholy air, wiping his mouth. There was catsup on his napkin like smears of lipstick.

Kelly said, "You must have to do a lot of official things, on holidays, don't you?—most of the time? Give speeches, accept awards—"

The Senator shrugged indifferently. "It's a lonely life, hearing your own voice in your ears so much."

"Lonely!" Kelly laughed.

But The Senator was saying, speaking quickly as if confiding in her, and not wanting her to interrupt, "It makes me angry sometimes, it's a visceral thing—how you come to despise your own words in your ears not because they aren't genuine, but because they *are*; because you've said them so many times, your 'principles,' your 'ideals'—and so damned little in the world has changed because of them." He paused, taking a large swallow of his drink. The tension in his jaws did in fact suggest anger. "You hate yourself for your putative 'celebrity': for the very reason others adore you."

And this too flattered Kelly Kelleher enormously for it seemed, didn't it, that, in speaking of such things, of such *others*, The Senator was excluding Kelly Kelleher from censure.

He was separated from his wife, his children were grown—her age, at least. Where was the harm?

She was explaining to her parents that they had only kissed, a single time. Where was the harm?

G—— had given her an infection of the genital-urinary tract but it was not one of the serious infections, it was not one of the unspeakable infections, it had disappeared months ago thanks to an antibiotic regimen. Where was the harm?

That morning, she'd bathed luxuriously in a peppermint-green sudsy water, carbonated bath tablets, "ActiBath," which Buffy had insisted she try.

They'd driven to town, to Grayling Harbor on the western side of the island, to stock up for the party. Harbor Liquor, The Fish Mart, Tina Maria Gourmet Foods, La Boulangerie. In front of La Boulangerie a shiny new Ford jeep was parked and on its rear bumper was the sticker THERE ARE NO POCKETS IN A SHROUD.

Distractedly, Buffy told Kelly as they were emerging from one or another of the stores, laden with expensive purchases, "Y'know—I don't know anyone who has died of AIDS since January first. I just realized."

Driving back to the cottage Buffy mentioned casually that Ray Annick had invited The Senator up for the party. But it wasn't the first time Ray had invited the man—"I don't expect him, really. *I* don't."

"Here? He's invited here?" Kelly asked.

"Yes, but I'd die if he showed up."

Also for the carbonated bubble-bath Buffy had pressed upon Kelly a new Spirit Music CD, "Dolphin Dreams." The sound was a soothing blend of dolphin song and choral voices, for the reduction of stress; but Kelly had not played it.

They'd missed the 7:30 P.M. ferry but they were not going to miss the 8:20 P.M. ferry. The Senator seemed annoyed, impatient. Staring at his watch, which was a digital watch, the numerals flashing like nerve tics. During their final hour at the party The Senator's mood shifted. He was not so coherent in his speech as he'd been, nor so fluent with repartee; he regarded Kelly Kelleher with that look familiar to her yet indefinable—a masculine proprietary look, edged with anxiety, indignation.

As they were leaving The Senator asked Kelly did she want one for the road, and Kelly said no, and The Senator said, would she take one for him, please?—apart from his own, that is, which he was carrying. At first Kelly thought he might be joking, but he wasn't: he had a newly freshened vodka-and-tonic in hand, and he wanted Kelly to bring a second. Kelly hesitated, but only for a moment.

Buffy caught up with Kelly in the driveway, squeezed her hand, whispered in her ear, "Call me, sweetie! Anytime tomorrow."

Meaning that it had not happened yet for there stood Buffy in the driveway staring after them her hand raised in a wan farewell.

32

IT HAD NOT HAPPENED YET, SHE SAW HERSELF DEFI-
antly running in her little white anklet socks on
the prickly carpet toes twitchy and wriggly and
someone tall swooping up behind her seizing
her beneath the arms tight and secure gripping
her beneath the armpits holding her safe *Who's
this! who's this! little angel-bee 'Lizabeth!*

That was so. She'd come that way. That was
the way she had come.

She saw that. There was no mistake. Yet at
the same time she was explaining to a gathering
of people, elders, whose faces were indistinct
through the cracked windshield that it was not
what they thought he had not abandoned her,

he'd gone to get help for her, that man whose name she could not recall, nor could she summon back his face though she was certain she would recognize it when she saw it, he had gone to get help to call an ambulance that was where he'd gone, he had not abandoned her to die in the black water.

He had not kicked her, he had not fled from her. He had not forgotten her.

Absurd pink-polished nails, now broken, torn. But she would fight.

A blood-flecked froth in her nostrils, her eyes rolling back in her head *but she would fight.*

... had not abandoned her kicking free of the doomed car swimming desperate to save his life to shore there lying exhausted vomiting the filthy water which no power on earth could induce him to return to, rising at last (after how long, he could not have said: a half-hour? an hour?) to flee on foot limping ignominiously *one shoe on*, *one shoe off* a singsong curse his enemies might one day chant if he could not prevent it, limping and stumbling back along the marshland road in terror of being discovered by a passing motorist back to the highway two miles away shivering convulsively his breath in panicked gasps *What can I do! What can I do! God instruct me what can I do!* the shrill mad cries of the insects and a nightmare sea of mosquitoes whining circling his head stinging his flesh that was so tender, swollen, his bruised forehead, his nose he believed must be broken striking with such force against the steering wheel, and at the highway he crouched panting like a dog crouched in hiding in the tall rushes waiting for traffic to clear so he could run limping across the road to an outdoor telephone booth in the parking lot of Post Beer & Wine dry-mouthed and numb in the protraction of visceral panic, the dreamlike protraction of a horror so unspeakable and so unacceptable it could not be contemplated but only fled, The Senator fleeing on foot *one shoe on, one shoe off* disheveled as a drunk and if anyone saw him? recognized him? photographed him? and if God Who had so long favored him now withdrew His favor? and if this ignominy was the end? limping gasping for breath covered in filthy black muck the end? and if he would not be redeemed one day exalted above his enemies and admirers alike? and if never nominated by his party after all, and if never elected president of the United States after all? and if cast down in derision in shame and the mockery of his enemies? for politics is in its essence as Adams had said *the systematic organization of hatreds*: either you were organized or you were not: the terror of it washing over him, sick, sick in his guts, swaying like a drunk running across the highway

though now fully sober and he would remain
sober he believed, he vowed, for the rest of his
life and it would be a good life if only God
would favor him now in this hour of anguish *If
You would have mercy now* wincing and dou-
bled over wracked with sudden pain in his bow-
els as somewhere close by in a municipal park
sparkling rockets shot into the night sky gaily
explosive and lurid in pinwheel colors RED
WHITE and BLUE and there trailed in the rockets' wake ooohs! and ahhhs! of childlike admira-
tion, a dog's sudden hysterical yipping and a
young man's furious yell "Shut it!" so it was not
gunshot but simply noise of no consequence
and he had a coin in his stiff fingers like a magi-
cal talisman, wallet snug in his pocket and
money in wallet intact, in fact hardly dampened
it seemed, he was able to speak calmly re-
questing directorial assistance calling the residence of St. John, Derry Road, gratified that he
could remember the name and there on the
eighth ring a woman answered and in the background a din of party voices so she had to ask
him to repeat himself, with whom did he want
to speak?—telling her, this stranger who was a
lifeline to him as a mere straw would be to a
man submerged in water just covering his head
in a slightly thickened, lowered voice of no dis-
cernible accent Ray Annick please, this is Gerald

Ferguson calling Ray Annick please and the
woman went away and the din of voices and
laughter increased and finally Ray was on the
line edgy, apprehensive, "Yeah? Gerry? What is
it?" knowing it must be trouble, for Ferguson
was no friend but a legal associate who would
never have called Ray Annick at such a time
unless it was trouble, and The Senator said in
his own voice faltering, desperate, "Ray, it isn't
Ferguson, it's me," and Ray said dumbly, *"You?"*
and The Senator said, "It's me and I'm in bad
trouble, there was an accident," and Ray asked,
with the faint falling air of a man reaching out
to support himself, "What? What accident?" and
The Senator said, his voice now rising, "I don't
know what the fuck I'm going to do: that girl—
she's dead," banging his already bruised forehead against the filthy Plexiglas wall of the telephone booth, so there was an instant's shocked
silence and then Ray said, "Dead——!" more an
inhalation of breath than an expletive, and then
he said, quickly, "Don't tell me over the phone!
Just tell me where you are and I'll come get
you," and The Senator was sobbing now, furious
and incredulous and aggrieved, "The girl was
drunk, and she got emotional, she grabbed at
the wheel and the car swerved off the road and
they'll say manslaughter, they'll get me for——"
and Ray interrupted, now angrily, with author-

ity, "Don't! Stop! Just tell me where you are for Christ's sake, and I'll come get you." And so The Senator did.

The digital numerals of his Rolex still flashing: 9:55 P.M.

But none of this Kelly Kelleher knew or could know for it seemed to her that in fact the accident had not happened yet—for there was the shiny black Toyota only now turning off the highway onto the desolate rutted road, the bright romantic moon above, something low and jazzy on the radio and, yes, she knew this was a mistake, probably a mistake, yes probably they were *lost* . . . but *lost* was their intention.

As the black water filled her lungs, and she died.

No: at the last possible moment coughing and choking she strained to lift her torso higher, to raise her head higher straining so that the small muscles stood out from the sinews and bone of her left arm as her fingers gripped what she no longer quite understood was the steering wheel but knew it was a device to save her for there was the bubble floating above shrunken now from its original size but it was there and she was all right hugging a startled Buffy St. John hard, hard, vowing she loved her like a sister and was sorry she had so deliberately shut herself off from Buffy these past two or three years telling her it was an accident, no one to blame.

And, yet, *had* it happened ...? The car speeding skidding along the road that seemed to have no houses, no traffic only swampy land stretching for miles everywhere the spiky brown rushes, the swaying tall grasses, stunted pines, so many strangely lifeless trees—treetrunks— and the harsh percussive rhythm of the insects' cries in their mating as if sensing how time accelerated, how the moon would shortly topple from the sky turned upside down and Kelly saw without registering she saw (for she and The Senator were talking) in a shallow ditch beside the road a broken dinette table, the front wheel of an English racing bicycle, the headless naked body of a flesh-pink doll ... looking away from the doll not wanting to see the hole between the shoulders like a bizarre mutilated vagina where the head had been wrenched off.

You're an American girl you love your life.

You love your life, you believe you have chosen it.

She was drowning, but she was not going to drown. She was strong, she meant to put up a damned good fight.

And there was his anxious face floating on the other side of the windshield as again, after she'd come to think he had abandoned her, he was diving for her, tugging at the door so violently the entire car rocked, and how tall he was, how warmly bronze his tanned skin, taller than nearly any man Kelly had ever seen, his wide white smile filled with teeth, those frizzy-wiry hairs on his arms and his arms were solid, muscular, his right wrist as he'd mentioned perceptibly thicker than his left from squash, decades of a fierce commitment to squash, and she touched the expensive white-gold digital watch on the wrist noting its tightness, the band pinching the flesh. Bemused it seemed by his state-of-the-art Rolex he said something about subsequent generations having a new concept of time seeing numerals flash and wink and fly by in contrast to the past where you looked at the face of a clock and saw the circular route of the hours as a measurable space to be traveled if only forward.

And his strong fingers crushing hers. *Kelly is it?—Kelly?*

That day that morning she'd been jogging on the beach amid the dunes, wind in her hair and the sun blazing white and in the frothy surf were sandpipers with prominently spotted breasts and long thin beaks and those delicate legs teetering pecking in the wet sand and she'd smiled at them, their curious scurrying movements, the oblivion of their concentration, feeling her heart swell *I want to live, I want to live forever!*

She was bargaining yes all right she would

trade her right leg, even both her legs if they thought it necessary, the emergency rescue team, yes amputate, all right please go ahead, please just do it she would sign the release later, she promised not to sue.

Artie Kelleher was the one!—for that was his character, "litigious" as the family teased him, but Kelly would explain the circumstances, Kelly would take the blame.

She was swallowing the black water in quick small mouthfuls reasoning that if she swallowed it quickly enough she would be simply drinking it, she would be all right.

What was that?—for her?—staring in blinking astonishment and elation at what Grandma had sewed her, a dress in white pucker-cotton printed with tiny strawberries, she would wear it with her new black patent-leather shoes and the white cotton anklet socks trimmed in pink.

You love the life you've lived because it is yours. Because that is the way you have come.

She saw them watching her closely, she had to hide her tears, not wanting them to be upset. Not wanting them to know.

Grandma, Mommy, Daddy—I love you.

Yet strange to her, not altogether pleasant, that they were so young. She had not remembered them so young.

It was risky it was the adventure of her

young life very likely yes probably a mistake but she'd leaned forward on her bare straining toes taking the kiss as if it were her due, for she was the one, she and none other, supplanting all the others, the young women who would have taken that kiss, from him, from that man whose name she had forgotten, in just that way.

She wasn't in love but she would love him, if that would save her.

She'd never loved any man, she was a good girl but she would love that man if that would save her.

The black water was splashing into her mouth, into her nostrils, there was no avoiding it, filling her lungs, and her heart was beating in quick erratic lurches laboring to supply oxygen to her fainting brain where she saw so vividly jagged needles rising like stalagmites—what did it mean? Laughing ruefully to think how many kisses she'd had tasting of beer? wine? whiskey? cigarettes? marijuana?

You love the life you've lived, there is no other.

You love the life you've lived, you're an American girl. You believe you have chosen it.

And yet: he *was* diving into the black water, diving to the car, his fingers outspread on the cracked windshield and his hair lifting in tendrils, *Kelly?—Kelly?*—she saw him mute and astonished and how many minutes, hours, had passed, how long had she been in this place she could not know for time would not move forward in this snug black corner trapped in the twisted metal in the clamp that held her fast. But she saw him!—there he was!—suddenly above her and swimming down to wrench open the door at last, the very door that had trapped her, and her heart swelled with joy and gratitude dangerously close to bursting as her eyes too strained from their sockets she lifted her arms to him, giving herself up to him so his strong fingers could close about her wrists and haul her up out of the black water at last! at last! rising together soaring suddenly so very easily weightless to the surface of the water and she slipped free of his hands like a defiant child eager to swim by herself now she was free kick-paddling with enormous relief her numbed legs restored to her as after a bad dream and with strong rhythmic strokes of her arms in the Australian crawl she'd been taught at school she bore herself triumphantly to the air above at last! at last! her dilated eyes seeing the splendid night sky restored to her again as if it had never been gone and the moon gigantic so shrewdly she thought *If I can see it, I am still alive* and that simple realization filled her with a great serene happiness seeing too Mommy and Daddy waiting amid the tall grasses though she was puzzled that now they were not young in fact but old, older than she knew, their faces haggard with grief staring in horror as if they had never seen her before in their lives, Kelly, little 'Lizabeth, as if they did not recognize her running there squealing in expectation in joy in her little white anklet socks raising her arms to be lifted high kicking in the air as the black water filled her lungs, and she died.

Acknowledgments

Data from "The Reimposition of Capital Punishment in New Jersey: The Role of Prosecutorial Discretion," by Leigh B. Bienen, Neil Alan Weiner, Deborah W. Denno, Paul D. Allison and Douglas Lane Mills, *Rutgers Law Review*, Fall 1988, and "This Is Your Death," by Jacob Weisberg, *The New Republic*, July 1, 1991, have been incorporated in chapter 30.

"Politics ... the systematic organization of hatreds," Henry Adams, *The Education of Henry Adams*, is quoted in chapter 32.